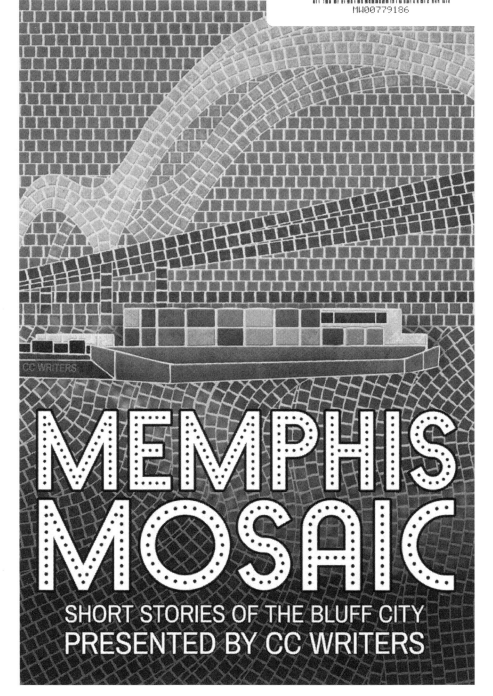

MEMPHIS MOSAIC

SHORT STORIES OF THE BLUFF CITY
PRESENTED BY CC WRITERS

Cover design by Beth Alvarez

ABOUT THIS BOOK

Memphis is a city steeped in history, culture, and vibrant storytelling. *Memphis Mosaic* celebrates the essence of the Bluff City through this collection of evocative and creative tales.

The original short stories in this anthology were written by members of Collierville Christian Writers, based in Collierville, Tennessee. Inspired by the rich heritage of West Tennessee, this diverse collection reflects the imagination and opinion of each writer.

Whether you're a lifelong Memphian or simply a visitor seeking to understand the city's soul, we hope this anthology offers a literary journey that will leave you inspired, intrigued, and entertained.

Annette Cole Mastron, Editor
Gary Fearon, Creative Director

CONTENTS

Many tiles are seen from above — some are

Empty, while others have colors amongst

Multitudes of spatial shapes; even more

Patterns turn to tales — rendered, sketched, or brushed.

Hovering low, we see sites, pivotal:

Islands and lakes; bridges with histories;

Statues and tombstones; tall buildings, next to

old mansions — and then, we hear the stories.

Mostly people dwell in verbal sketches —

Ordinary folks — they will work, play, strive,

Struggle, and grow; there may be dilemmas

And loss, but still laughs and love in their lives.

In the end, it's not *where* — it's *who* masters

Challenges along the mosaic's shores.

John Burgette

THE COLOR OF GRIEF
Beth Alvarez

It took ten months of working three jobs before I could afford it, but the car was mine. The first new vehicle I'd ever owned—or, that I would own, after another 53 monthly payments.

Rain hammered the windshield like I was on my way to Memphis in May, but I wasn't. For one, it was late July, and as I pulled into a parking lot beside where a flatbed tow truck dragged a sleek black sedan up its back—a car far more expensive than my little 60-payments-at-7%-interest number—I hit the button on my phone to let my rider know I was there.

Two years of saving, and the only reason I could afford the stupid thing was because I'd started a side gig doing ride sharing.

The tow driver and the man I assumed had requested a ride stood on the sidewalk under a wide black umbrella, watching the car creep upward as the winch whirred and its chain clacked. Normally, I never knew who I was there to pick up. The suitcase on the ground beside his legs was the giveaway.

I wasn't required to get out and help, but if the guy didn't respond to the notification that I was there within a reasonable time, the ride would be canceled, and I needed the cash. The silent choice between poking my head out the window or just honking played out for longer than I liked.

The latter won.

The tow guy flinched at the horn, but the old man holding the umbrella barely turned his head. He checked his pocket—his phone, I assumed—and adjusted something held under his arm before he turned to pick up his suitcase.

Yep. That was him.

I stepped out to greet him, half expecting he'd need help to put his luggage in the trunk, but he was stronger than I would have guessed and had no difficulty carrying his things on his own.

3

"Sam, I presume?" His voice was as smooth as a rake scraping concrete.

I offered my best smile as I hit the button to pop the trunk. "Yep, I'm your ride. Need a hand?"

"I have two of my own, thank you." He swung the suitcase into the trunk. The shocks shuddered under the sudden weight. The brown paper *something* stayed under his arm.

Flowers. Bright pink. Well, that made sense; I was supposed to be taking him to a cemetery. I opened one of the back doors as he slammed the trunk. Most people sat in back. They preferred it that way. I always figured it made it feel more like a real taxi, but maybe it was that the distance between us made me a little less human.

"Here for a funeral?" My voice shook a little, though I tried to be casual. Death wasn't casual, and the old man wore a black suit. A suit and a round little hat like you'd see on a piano player in an old western saloon—or at least, the kind in movies. Bandits and outlaws had a good life in those. Maybe next time I needed a car, I'd just rob a train.

His mouth crinkled tight as he climbed in back and tilted his umbrella to shake off the rain before he closed it. "Just a visit, thank you."

In this weather? I glanced at the sky. "Ah. I just figured you were dressed for it." I didn't know if the cemetery would hold funerals in the pelting rain. Heck, I hadn't known there *was* a cemetery out where we were headed. I climbed back into the driver's seat and was glad for the leather. It was far more forgiving of the rain than cloth seats would have been.

"Is that so?" The old man sounded amused.

"The black suit and all that," I explained as I backed out of the lot and pulled onto Stage.

"Just business attire, I'm afraid, even if it's appropriate. Though, you know, mourning clothes are white in some countries."

I didn't know. Traditional funeral attire from around the world had never been one of my interests. "That so?" I glanced at the rear-view mirror, but all I could see was the bouquet of bright pink

4

flowers hovering beside the back of my seat. "I thought the color of grief was always black."

The silence that followed was oddly heavy. The weight of it made my spine itch, but I told myself it was just a raindrop prickling its way down my back as I squirmed.

I checked the GPS on my phone and stole a glimpse of the old man as I looked behind me and changed lanes. There was something painful carved into the lines of his craggy face, something I'd seen before, though I couldn't place when.

Either way, it was clear the funeral talk had been a bad choice.

I cleared my throat and tried again. Cordial drivers were the ones who got tips. "So, where are you headed after this? You got a hotel or something?"

"I suppose I shall have to find one. The automotive dealership has promised to call me when my vehicle is ready." The way the guy talked was as old-fashioned as his hat, but there was something charming about it, too. In another place, another time, it might have been fun to hear his story.

"There are some places by the mall that are nice but not too expensive," I suggested. "Right around the corner from the cemetery. I can look up the phone number for one once we park, if you want."

"I would prefer if you take me there directly once my business is concluded."

"Ah, I don't think I can do that. I'll need to go find my next ride. They keep us hopping, and Wolfchase is a pretty busy area." I needed the money, too. Car payment aside, there was rent to think of, and nowhere was cheap anymore.

The old man made a sound that reminded me of my sister's grumpy cat. "My luggage is already in your trunk, and it would be unkind to make a man of my age lift it more than once. I shan't be long, and I will make the wait worth your while."

I hesitated.

"Cash," he added.

No further persuasion needed. "Hey, you take however long you need." I'd just let the meter run, hang out in the car while he placed his flowers, then get him to add the hotel as a stop. No problem. It wasn't like pit stops were against the rules, they just usually weren't worth the dough.

He added nothing else to the conversation and it wasn't long before we swung onto the cemetery's narrow lane.

Or, the lane where my phone's map said the cemetery was supposed to be. I saw the sign—Shelby County Cemetery—but beyond that, there was nothing. No standing headstones. Just an empty, sprawling field. My palms slid up the steering wheel as I inched past the white fencing that framed the entrance. "Is this right?"

"Yes. It isn't far, so you may park here. You may join me, if you wish." Already, the old man had his umbrella in one hand and the pink bouquet in the other.

Considering the rain, joining him was the last thing I wanted to do. Then I considered the cash tip he'd already promised and reevaluated my reluctance to help. "I can hold your umbrella, if you want."

He offered a thoughtful hum in response and stepped from the car. I met him on the rough pavement and swung the big black umbrella over our heads as we walked. The rain-soaked earth squished under my canvas hi-tops and I tried not to worry about cleaning them. The old man seemed to know where he was going, despite the lack of headstones.

"Where are the graves?" I asked, no louder than a whisper. I hadn't meant to be quiet, but something choked me, as if the emptiness of the field around us had stolen my voice.

The old man pointed down. All I saw were muddy metal disks in the ground. Dozens of them, row after row, packed so close together I thought I might span the gap between them with my shoe.

"Have you any children, Sam?" The old man's voice was calm, steady, but the simple question shook me to the core. It was obvious why he was asking, why the graves were so close together and the markers so small. The realization of what we walked across felt like a punch in the gut.

I tried to sound casual anyway. "I've got three jobs and a payment on a new car," And no time for dates, much less parenthood. "But, uh, maybe someday."

"Then I shall hope you are blessed with a someday, and that yours proves to last a little longer." He stopped at a marker that was no different to my eyes, but etched with a number I knew was etched on his heart.

I didn't know what to say. Sure, I'd lost people—plenty of them. But never like this.

The old man knelt beside the dirty marker and pulled the cone of flowers from its brown paper bag. The ground was soft from all the rain and the spike at its tip sank deep. Then he slid his thumb across the old metal disk to wipe it clean.

"I've changed my mind," he said as he rubbed his thumb against his fingers, letting the crust of mud fall away in pills. "I believe I will stay here for a while. Leave my suitcase on the asphalt, if you will. I'll call another for a ride when I am ready."

"Are you sure?" Ride fare scarcely crossed my mind. I didn't want to leave him in the rain. Not like this. Not alone, far from home, drawn back by a pain I could never understand.

But it was clear he'd made his decision, because he pulled his wallet from the pocket of his neatly pressed trousers and drew out the crispest bills I'd seen in years. "Yes. Thank you for your time and patience."

Guilt coursed over me at the thought of taking the cash from his fingertips. I couldn't do it. Not here, not with the one thing his money couldn't buy resting forever under my feet. I didn't know his story. I didn't think I wanted to know. But places like this weren't happy memories, and the tiny gap between the markers was dwarfed by the size of the loss buried beneath each number.

I swallowed hard and pushed the money back into his hand, then gave him his umbrella, too. "I'll bring your stuff over here, so you don't have to keep an eye on it."

He did not protest, just folded the bills into the palm of his hand and let the shaft of the umbrella rest against his shoulder.

Mud squished under my uncomfortably wet hi-tops all the way

back to my car, then all the way back to the gravesite. I took a second to end the ride, then shut off the ride share app. After whatever had just transpired, I didn't think I could work right now.

The old man thanked me for the suitcase, but he did not rise or say goodbye. He just stayed where he was, with the burnt ochre of the Memphis mud soaking his knees.

I tried to think of something to say, but everything stuck in my throat, so I just turned to go. I only made it a few steps.

"Tell me, Sam," he called after me. "What is the color of grief?"

The colors were everywhere, now that I looked. In the little blue car left by another nameless marker, in the yellow ribbon on a teddy bear's neck as it sat watching over a metal pin, in the cheerful pink flowers he'd left as a tribute—and in the bold red beads of my Abuela's rosary, hanging over the rear-view mirror of my car.

"I don't know," I answered, but now it was a lie.

The color of grief was everywhere, and it was the color of life.

NOT MY DAY
Barbara Ragsdale

Underneath my bed is the repository for all the old family pictures no one else wants. I love to look at them. But there are no names, places, or dates. They are somebody's memories, but whose?

When I ask my sister, "Who is that?" she responds with "I think it's…" just as confused as I am.

I separate them into two stacks labeled: *before me and after me.* The girls with corseted slim waists, billowing sleeves, and hair piled high on their heads, like the Gibson Girls, are definitely before me.

The tintypes are brittle and fragile. My maternal grandmother stands beside a stern elderly man seated in a chair with a trouser leg folded up under him. She has long curly hair, high-top button shoes, a ruffled dress and a big bow sash tied around her waist. She is lovely.

I rummage around and pull out from the bottom a tattered

black and white snapshot. The picture tears at my heart. It pulls away the curtain of memories and, suddenly, I'm back to 1943, the house by the railroad track and the war years.

I have to squint to find Annie in the picture. She is seated in the shadows. Her rich brown skin blends into the shaded background. My emotions are captured by her eyes. They stare back at me with hidden thoughts. It's a brooding scene, a troubling scene. It speaks of social norms and practices that I knew so little about at the time.

∾

Annie arrived late that morning. No doubt one of the two buses she must ride was delayed. It was a constant struggle. The buses were rarely on time. She sat in the back of the bus as dictated by signs and customs. On cold days the back of the bus was warmer, out of the way from the doors that opened and let in a blast of frigid air.

Annie lived in a tiny shotgun house in a historic community. I know because we drove her home many times. There are dirt roads, few utilities, but a unique history. A developer bought land from a plantation to create a neighborhood for black home ownership and called the settlement Orange Mound. Lots sold for $40 and were 25 feet wide and 100 feet deep. To my surprise, Annie was an owner.

Each day she walks the few blocks of dirt road from her home to the bus stop. Standing on a street corner meant being subjected to the elements which bordered on insanity. Hot one day, cold the next and rain in between.

On this school morning I raced out the front door and flew past Annie. My light jacket flapping in the breeze. "Hi, Annie. Bye, Annie," and give her a hug.

The early morning air felt crisp and cool. One of those Southern days when the temperature went from a frosty forty degrees to sunny and warm in the seventies by noon.

"Margaret left early and John drove," I yelled in passing. John had an old two-seater convertible with a rumble seat. It was loud and subject to flat tires. Annie was terrified to ride in it. "Daddy says we are going to the Pink Palace. Want to go?" I threw out the question while racing to the street.

Annie shrugged her shoulders. She trudged along the long stretch of walkway leading from the sidewalk to the screened porch. Never one for many words, she smiled as I rushed past. She told me once, "I didn't get to go to school."

Annie was there to help Mother with laundry. I didn't like laundry day. It was back-breaking work.

She paused to watch as I ran to meet my friends. "See ya later. Gotta meet Koran at the railroad track." We had to cross the track before a train came or we would be late for school. Two years into the war and troop trains ran day and night. Young men waved and yelled out the windows.

Annie wore a round-brimmed cloth hat that was flattened to her head. It fit snug over her dark hair sprinkled with gray. Her walk a slow gait from a touch of arthritis in her hips. She wiped away a sheen of perspiration across her forehead. Deep lines etched her face to give her plump cheeks.

She grasped her coat around her slim body. Her arms cradled the paper sack she always carried. It held a myriad of things. I never knew quite what she protected except the small brown sack holding a glass bottle. "What's that?" I asked.

"Never you mind," she chided. "That's between me and Mister John." Mister John being my father.

I rushed home after school. Quickly changed the school dress for shorts and tossed it all into the dirty clothes basket. I grabbed my skates stuffed in the corner of the closet. Slung them over my shoulder and stuffed the key in my pocket. I could spend hours skating up and down the sidewalk.

Annie was in the kitchen struggling with the old wringer washer. She'd mutter to herself, shaking her head, "Put on; take off, put on; take off." My sister was a high-school teenager who constantly changed outfits. I didn't worry about clothes.

The machine was shoved to the back porch out of the way until wash day. Then Mother pulled, and Annie pushed the awkward contraption over the threshold toward the sink. Fortunately, it was on wheels. A black rubber hose had to be hooked up for the hot and cold faucets.

It was a cumbersome piece of equipment, but easier and faster than a tub and washboard. "What's the matter, Annie?"

"Sheet caught in the roller and wound around," she mumbles trying to unwrap a bed sheet caught between the twin rollers.

"Can I help?" peering down into the tub to see how much of the laundry was left. I could see it was almost finished. The rollers squeeze out the water before hanging wet clothes outside to dry. Annie is careful that her arms don't get pulled in and smashed between the rollers.

"Not now," she answered. "It's about loose." She rubs her back to relieve the discomfort from wrestling all the clothes. It's bend and stretch to do laundry. Outside, Mother folds the dried wash and drops everything into a basket. My dog Sandy races around. She knows I'm home from school.

I open the fridge to chip ice off the big hunk. The ice pick, sharp and deadly, slices a chunk that I stab again to make smaller. Tea, already sweetened, is in a pitcher. Just needs ice and lemon.

"About the Pink Palace. We're going tomorrow. I'm not sure what that is, but do you want to go?" Annie turns to face me. Her dark eyes fill with sadness and her shoulders slump forward.

"Wrong color. Not my day," she answers softly. I don't understand.

"Why? What do you mean?" I sip the tea, puzzled. I thought any day was visiting day for the Palace.

She struggles to answer. "Ask Mr. John. He knows." Annie joins me at the small kitchen table. She relaxes her breath, weary from wrestling with the sheet stuck between the rollers.

"Uh... Okay, I'll ask Daddy." I put the empty tea glass on the counter by the sink. "And I'll tell you all about it when we get home."

Annie doesn't work every day, but after wash day, the next day is for ironing. Clothes are sprinkled with water overnight so that wrinkles can be ironed out.

We left soon after lunch the next day and spent most of the afternoon at the museum. Margaret and I wore hats with flaps over the ears. Terrible looking. John resembled a *hep* young man. The front brim of his hat turned up.

While we were gone, Annie ironed. She's in the kitchen bending over the board shoving a hot iron back and forth over a tablecloth. The room feels stuffy. The basket of sprinkled clothes from the night before is almost empty. She looks tired.

I'm full of news. "It's called the Pink Palace because it's built of pink and gray marble, and it's huge." Annie looks interested but subdued. "There are a lot of stuffed animals, lions, bears and more. One Polar Bear stands with a raised paw. He looks scary. Mostly we walked and walked. Daddy took some pictures. It was cold outside.

"Marble stairs go to the second floor. I could hear my shoes click on the floor. There were big paintings on the walls. They are wonderful." Annie listened and added "un-huh" occasionally.

In later years, I would learn the historical significance of the home turned into a museum. Clarence Saunders, a visionary in retail grocery operations and founder of the Piggly Wiggly chain, began the exotic home for his wife. Its arched front is sided with long wings on each side. Due to a financial battle with Wall Street, Saunders eventually lost the home before completion.

The incomplete home was donated to the city of Memphis along with ten acres of land and the city renovated it as a museum. Berry Brooks, a big-game hunter, went to Africa and Asia on hunting expeditions. He contributed preserved trophies from those trips to the museum. Eventually a room was named after him.

Other exhibits detailed Memphis history in agriculture, cotton, and Blues on Beale. Tall murals on the second floor of the home were done by Burton Callicott, a local artist, and part of the Works Progress government art project during the Depression.

Saunders made and lost more than one fortune. His vision for a fully automated grocery system called "The Keydoozle" was 50 years before its time. He opened three stores. The failure was not due to the concept. It happened because the infrastructure wasn't available. People flocked to the stores, but errors in filling orders and equipment malfunctions doomed the innovative ideas.

I went on and on telling Annie about what we had seen at The Pink Palace. She tried to be interested. Through the years we had many conversations around the kitchen table. Mostly, I talked, and Annie listened until I asked her a specific question. "Annie, where were you born?" I heard her gasp. She wheeled around to stare at me.

She drew a deep breath before she answered. "In a shack. In the middle of a cotton field." Her words were harsh. I'd never heard Annie show any kind of anger.

"Okay, but I don't know where that is. I was born in Arkansas. Where was your shack?" Like a lot of children, I didn't know when to quit asking unwanted questions.

She sighed a painful breath of air. "In Alabama. It was a long time ago. Nothing left there now." Annie lifted herself slowly from the chair. She disappeared into the small pantry where her paper sack rested on the floor. I could hear the rattle. She sipped from the small bottle and then twisted the cap back on. She went back to finish the laundry, lost in her thoughts.

Days later my brother announced wonderful news. "The Fairgrounds is open, Let's go." I loved going to the fun place that was home to the Barnum and Bailey circus when it came to town. Since we lived close to the railroad that brought the circus animals, I saw the elephants unload from the cars and lumber to the grounds to pull up the circus tents.

Once again I approached Annie about going.

"We're going to the to the Fairgrounds. Have you been? I like to ride the Tumblebug and the horses on the Carousel. I lean out and catch a brass ring. There's plenty of room in John's car. You can ride in the rumble seat." Annie looked frozen with fear.

She busies herself with dishes in the sink and stirs something on the stove.

"Not my day," she answers, a little louder, a sharper tone.

"Wrong color." The curious answer puzzled me even more.

"I don't understand."

"Ask Mr. John. He knows." My brother passes by.

"Be quiet, Bobbie," he said. "You ask too many questions."

I stomped out of the room. "I just want to know when it is her day."

"Shut up," he growls.

"Mother says not to use those words." I argue back.

"Well then…. stop talking," and he bounds up the stairs to his room.

Segregation meant little to me at age ten. A life of advantage versus one without was not a concept that I fully understood.

We spent hours at the Fairgrounds running from one ride to another, waiting in line for tickets.

At home, tired and hungry after the trip, I slapped a sandwich together and told Annie about all we had done. "Oh, Annie, the Fairgrounds was the most fun. John rode the roller coaster five times. Margaret yelled from the top of the Farris Wheel. I was too scared to ride either of them, but I couldn't anyway. I was too small. I rode a horse."

"A real horse?" she twisted around in shock.

I laughed. "No, Annie. It was the Carousel that goes round and round. They are painted horses. Bright, brilliant red and blue colors, on poles that move up and down. There are beautiful carriages where people sit. Organ music plays happy tunes the whole time."

I stuff my hand in a pocket to give her a present. "I brought you something," and give her a fistful of cotton candy. Sticky stuff wrapped in a napkin I'd stuck in my pocket. She reluctantly pinches a bit of the pink fluff for a taste.

"Good," she says and smiles as the sugar treat melts in her mouth.

Annie came on Saturday morning the next week. She usually only worked weekdays. Bus schedules were different on the weekend. Hard for her to get to the house. If Daddy asked her to help with Sunday dinner, John would pick her up and drive her home. Annie took the food home.

Daddy walked into the kitchen where Annie was washing and drying the breakfast dishes. Her homemade apron covered her street dress. The ever-present hat was perched on top of her head. "Annie, we're going to Johnny Mills Barbecue for lunch," he said. "You can ride in the back and hold Bobbie."

I heard him and blurted out, "You mean it's her day and she can go." Daddy looked like he wanted to throttle me. Instead, he answered patiently.

"Yes, Annie can go."

"Why can she go there and not all those other places?" He stares back at me.

"Because Johnny Mills serves all customers. Even Bing Crosby has been there. We'll be leaving soon." He turned around and left the room. I was more confused than ever. Annie smiled.

Annie removed her apron and stuffed it in the sack. She washed her hands, smoothed her hat, and got ready to go. The trip took a long time. All the way downtown. But the barbecue was worth it. The aroma of cooking pork filled the air long before I could see the building.

I saw Daddy take Annie aside. "Here's the money for your sandwich or ribs. I'll let you know when we're ready to go home." Annie didn't sit with us while she ate.

Little black girls stood in the doorway between the two sides and sang. A hat rested on the floor in front of them and people dropped in money.

Johnny Mills Barbecue preceded almost all other similar restaurants, cooking the shoulders and ribs over charcoal. He lathered the meat continuously with a sweet spicy sauce. Mills started his business small in 1929, cooking in a pit near his home. By 1932 he had built his own brick building serving all who walked through the door. He even shipped his products to celebrities like Kate Smith. We ate out fill.

Before she went home, I heard Annie and Daddy talking. "Mr. John, I need your help."

"Okay. What about?"

"I want to register to vote. How do I do that?" Daddy looked startled. Annie stood quietly.

"Do you rent where you live" he asked.

Annie stretched up tall. "I own my home," she replied proudly.

"That's good. There may be a tax, a small amount. Can you read and write?"

"Yes. I read my Bible every night. Had to write when I worked in a grocery store."

Daddy looked thoughtful. "I'm not sure where you go to register, but I'll check."

"Thank you. I want to vote at least once before I die." Daddy nodded and slipped out of the room. He chose to keep to himself any negative events Annie might experience while trying to register.

"Ready to go home, Annie," John asked.

Annie donned her coat, positioned the hat again and grabbed her paper sack. John helped her into the back rumble seat. A big grin crossed his face. He loved the old car.

"Let's fly, Annie. Let's fly," he yelled.

Annie sat tall in the back seat. Her eyes were big and round as saucers. One arm had a death grip wrapped around her sack and the other clamped firmly on her hat to keep it from blowing away. I think she mumbled a prayer.

The river of memories is long and sometimes painful. The war invaded the family in 1943. The Army Air Force taught John to fly. Mr. John went overseas as a civilian employee with Lockheed. A neighbor's son was a POW for five years.

Those left at home survived rationing and bought Saving Stamps for bonds. Nobody knew anything about D-Day.

Annie registered to vote with no problem. Mr. John drove her to the site. I don't know if she lived to see the day when "any day was her day" at the Pink Palace and the Fairgrounds. Her picture remains with the family snapshots.

COURT SQUARE MAGIC
Karen Busler

"Hear ye, hear ye! The conclave of the cherubs of the goddess Hebe is called into session. It is safe to appear."

The iron cherubs, in various poses under the bowls of the huge fountain below the statue of the goddess Hebe in Court Square in downtown Memphis, seemed to come to life.

The head cherub, Jorey, announced, "The graced moment has come for us to welcome our goddess, Hebe, cup bearer to the gods, the goddess of youth and beauty, and daughter of Zeus and Hera, into our presence as was prescribed at the beginning."

Jorey blew his horn and all the cherubs bowed in their places. Hebe floated down from her high point on the fountain and appeared to them as in a mist. She was an ethereal, beautiful form, moving among them and touching each one which brought them to life.

Jorey stated to her, "It is time."

Her voice, seductive as a siren song, sang, "I am ready."

Jorey bowed deeply and Hebe merged back into her iron façade, waiting for the defining moment of her fate.

Discussion among the cherubs as to how to proceed began and a course of action was agreed upon. They knew there was only one chance at completing their predestined mission and it had to be done right or all would be lost.

If any human had heard them speaking, it would have sounded like a strange whooshing sound with no wind.

It was 1:00 in the morning and Richard couldn't wait to get home to his apartment balcony that overlooked Court Square and the fountain. It had been a long and satisfying day in his artist's studio, and sitting out in the warm, spring-scented night air with his favorite bourbon was a nightly indulgence he looked forward to more than he cared to admit. This night there wasn't even a stray cat around, and the intermittent vagrants had settled down for the night, making it easy to hear the soft breezes rustling the tree leaves as well as the current in the waters of the mighty Mississippi.

As he sipped his bourbon, he once again looked at the fountain. He knew this was a copy of the original, but that didn't diminish his admiration for the sculptor from more than a century ago. As an artist, he marveled at Hebe's smooth and shapely iron breasts, lithe arms, and flowing hair. "Maybe this was how the ancients immortalized their fabricated gods and goddesses," he said under his breath. "Not a bad way to do it."

"What was that?" He was startled at a different sound. "Are those sparks of light around the fountain?" He looked again intently. "It's probably just light reflecting on the water," he said to no one.

But it wasn't.

After a second drink Richard nodded off in his comfy balcony chair.

᪣

"Human, wake up!"

Richard swatted at his head as if there were a mosquito buzzing in his ear.

"Human, there isn't much time – WAKE UP!"

Richard waked with a start. "Heaven help me!" he cried as he shrank into his chair. "Who, *what* are YOU!?"

"Please calm down. I'm not going to hurt you," said the odd-looking metallic creature.

It was all Richard could do to breathe. Even in his wildest fantasies nothing like this had ever happened to him, and he was pretty sure he was awake and not dreaming.

"My name is Jorey. I'm the head cherub of the goddess Hebe, whom we serve," he said with a bow. "We have seen you admiring our mystical goddess and have come in this time and in this place to one human. We have chosen you."

Richard's mouth was dry and could hardly speak. He croaked out, "What do you want from me?" He was dumbfounded that he could hear and plainly understand this bizarre looking creature and thought, *Get a grip, man! This could be a golden opportunity, of what I don't know, but I'm going to find out.*

"Explain yourself," Richard said, pulling himself up to his full six foot height, towering over the little… whatever it was.

Jorey eyed the tall human, satisfied with what he saw and explained, "We are here to fulfill our mission to our goddess. To do that, a human must help us. This was decreed from the beginning and we've been watching and waiting for the right human at the right time, and that time is now, with you."

"Okay, you've got my attention – tell me more," Richard said cautiously.

Jorey smiled to himself. The initial meeting with the human was going well, but he pondered on how much to tell him. He didn't want this to fail at the beginning.

"We servants of Hebe are imploring you, a human admirer of our goddess, to help us free her from her station. She has been the cup bearer to the gods since she was created, bringing them the ambrosial nectar of youth, beauty, and immortality. We are offering you, a worthy human, to accept our offer of earthly youth, virility and longevity. You'll live life with pleasures you can't begin to fathom, with all the respect and dignity of Hebe's position."

Astonished, Richard looked at the metallic cherub and laughed.

"So you want me to give up my life as a human being and

become a god to take Hebe's place? Why would I do that? Can't she ditch her life as it is now and change into something else without me? If she's a goddess, she should be able to do that."

Jorey looked worried and, raising his head, looked Richard right in the eyes and said with a hypnotic voice, "You will do this. You will meet Hebe tomorrow night at this time."

And with that, the cherub-come-to-life was gone.

Richard stumbled to bed and slept hard. When he awoke, he thought, *Wow, what a wild dream that was. I've got to stop drinking so much late at night.* And with that self-admonition, he put his mind on his current painting and left for his studio to work.

All the cherubs crowded around Jorey when he returned from speaking with the human. "What did he say? Has he consented?"

Jorey reported unhappily, "He didn't jump at the chance and I had to use my magic on him to make him think this meeting was a dream. But he's primed, and I'm sure our goddess will convince him."

The cherubs all nodded in agreement that it was best for the human to have a little time to wrap his mind around the whole idea. It was very important to all the cherubs, and to Hebe, that this happen, otherwise, they would all be extinct like almost all the gods and goddesses of old.

Richard called his girlfriend the next morning from his studio, "Hey Julie, want to go to lunch? I have to tell you about the crazy dream I had last night."

"Okay, but you're buying," she teased with a grin because she knew he always insisted on paying.

A while later over ribs and beer, Richard recounted the whole night's happenings to her.

"That was some dream, Babe!" Julie said while shaking her head. "But wouldn't it be something if that were all true? What a hard decision to make, to be young and beautiful always and live forever, or not! What would you choose?"

Richard said, "I don't know. I've been distracted thinking about this whole idea all morning. But since it was just a dream it's not a decision I have to make."

⁓

Richard made it home that night, very late as usual, and vowed to have only one double bourbon to keep from having such bizarre dreams. He sat once again on his balcony, looking at the fountain and enjoying the night air. He was about to doze off when he saw the strangest thing – the fountain started spraying water, and lights coming from nowhere were dancing on the rippling surface of the pool below.

What's going on here? He thought. *They always shut off the fountain at night.* But he kept watching and the most beautiful sight he'd ever seen appeared to ascend from the top of the fountain.

He was enraptured by the vision – female in form, ethereal, with sparks of light and color flashing from the mist surrounding her in all directions. And it was coming right towards him, singing in the most mesmerizing way!

Richard nearly lost his mind when he heard that sound. *Where did that voice come from?* At least he assumed it was a voice. He stood and leaned over the rail to see and hear everything that was happening.

The iron cherub said Hebe would come to me tonight, he remembered. *If this really is Hebe, then I'm ready to go anywhere with her!*

The dazzling, ravishing form hovered in front of him, its beauty almost too much to bear.

She sang with her siren voice, "I'm here for you. Please do me the honor of accompanying me."

"Yes," was all he could say, and they disappeared to who knows where.

The cherubs all watched this until Hebe and Richard disappeared. They smiled among themselves and knew their plan was progressing tremendously. There was only one hurdle left, and it was a big one. The human had to drink the ambrosial nectar Hebe will offer him to guarantee that he will take her place, so they will all continue to exist. If he didn't drink it, then Hebe and all the cherubs would return to the ether from whence they came, never to be heard from again. Then the fountain would be a shell of its former self, made of cast iron, with no life in it ever again.

The next morning, Richard awoke in his own bed but was unsure of what had happened the night before. He looked in the bathroom mirror and even though he appeared the same, he felt different inside. Then he started to remember snippets of the previous night – the floating together with Hebe, going to her empty home where the gods used to live, experiencing vicariously what eternal youth, beauty, and life would be like. He knew this was no dream – this was real. He couldn't wait to be with Hebe again that night.

The day plodded on for Richard. Losing himself in his painting, which he normally loved, didn't happen, and every minute dragged on. All he could think about was Hebe and how he longed to be with her. He finally gave up and went home to wait for the night and the ecstasy that awaited him.

Jorey spoke to the cherubs on the final evening of this turning point in all their lives. "My fellow cherubs, we have fulfilled all the precepts to preserve the life of our beloved goddess, Hebe, and therefore our lives. Let us pray to the gods who are left that we will be victorious in our quest for life."

&

Richard took his bourbon out on the balcony and stared wistfully at Hebe atop the fountain, hoping it all wasn't a dream and that she would come for him again tonight. He didn't know what would happen, but he hadn't forgotten about the offer Jorey had made a mere two nights ago. To give up his humanity to live forever intrigued him – even though he knew his soul was already in its eternal life, so that really wasn't an issue. Although to be young, beautiful, and virile forever did appeal to him. But as in all mysteries, he was sure there were parts of this offer that weren't known to him, and he was also sure they weren't good.

He knew he was helpless when it came to being with Hebe, but he prayed to God, the real God, to help him through this.

At the appointed time the vision of rapture began. Richard stood and watched the cherubs, led by Jorey, make a pathway for Hebe to come to him. She surrounded him with her loveliness and once again, they disappeared. Jorey said to the cherubs, "It's all in our goddess's hands now," and they bowed their heads and waited.

&

Hebe and Richard found themselves once again in her deserted home.

"Where are all the other gods and goddesses," he asked.

She sang plaintively, "They were unsuccessful in convincing a human to take their places so they are no more."

He was sorry for that, but he wanted Hebe to remain since he was completely enchanted by her. She prepared a crystal goblet of the youth-giving ambrosial nectar for him to drink and offered it to him. He took it, and looking into it, he saw his life up until now in the liquid. This was a sobering moment, seeing all the joys and sorrows of his life.

He asked her if drinking this would keep her alive and she sang her most alluring and beautiful siren song yet. "Yes," she sang, and grew more brilliantly dazzling than before. He couldn't keep his eyes off her – her radiance was beyond breathtaking. He lifted the cup to his lips but before he drank, he remembered to pray again to God to do the right thing.

At that moment, there was a distant sound like thunder and a tremor under his feet that shook him out of his trance. He dropped the goblet and it shattered into tiny shards as the nectar flew into the air and dissipated.

"NOOOOOO!!" Hebe cried, her siren's voice broken. The look on her gorgeous face was that of painful resignation. She had failed in her quest, and the human mortal was exempt from taking over her life as a forgotten goddess, which would have freed her to live with her kind in another realm. Wrenched out of his stupor, Richard's mind was keenly aware that he had been rescued from a horrendous mistake and grateful to God for saving him.

Instantly he was back on his balcony, his small glass of bourbon on the table next to his chair, and keenly aware of all that had transpired. He looked at the fountain and saw shimmering lights swirling around the waters, and he knew it was the end for Hebe and her cherubs. The lights exploded like fireworks as each cherub went into nothingness, with Hebe being the last in one glorious cascade of glitter into oblivion. He was devastated that she was gone, but still grateful that he had not changed the course of his natural life.

The fountain went dark, and the sound of trickling water was all that was heard.

❧

After a night on his knees in prayers of thanksgiving to God and intermittent tortured sleep, Richard swore off the bourbon and decided to move far away from the fountain, even though he knew it would never tempt him or anyone else again. He simply didn't need the reminder of Hebe and the events that happened here.

❧

Richard woke up the next day with dried sweat all over him. He wondered why he felt so wrung out — as if he'd run a marathon in his sleep. He got his coffee and went out on the balcony, ready to enjoy the morning air, except it was already a bustling mid-afternoon. He couldn't believe he'd slept that long. Something must be wrong with him.

He settled in his chair and looked out over Court Square and gazed at the fountain with all the pedestrians and vagrants and pigeons around it. The fountain looked the same as always - there was nothing different about it, but somehow it had lost its allure for him.

He sighed and thought, *Maybe I'm just tired of it, but that couldn't be it. It's like all the life has gone out of it, but it's not a living thing so how could that be?*

It was strange how bereft he felt that morning. But his life was good and he chalked it up to a night of exhausting dreams.

He shook it off and thought, *Things will be fine once I get back to work.*

Richard showered and, feeling refreshed, went to his studio to paint. He had an unexpected idea, picked up his brush, and started creating something extraordinary. He painted a hauntingly beautiful woman, clothed in a mist of sparkling light and color, hovering in the air and beckoning the viewer to come with her.

He had no clue where this idea had come from, but he was

delighted with it. Every day when he took the cover off the canvas, he felt as if he were unveiling his soul. Little did he know that he was given the immense grace of not remembering any of the events of those pivotal three nights. He would never know that this masterpiece was inspired by the distant memory of the goddess herself, which still resided in his deepest subconscious.

Hebe was gone forever, but her eternally suppressed memory was making a huge difference in Richard's life, including gallery exhibitions, fame, and fortune. In a way, Hebe did give him the gift of youth, beauty, and vitality by giving him the inner vision to see and paint ravishing beauty that no one else could see except through his work.

He endlessly marveled at this change in himself and painted like a man possessed – creating painting after painting inspired by his Artistic Muse, as he now called her. It was this forgotten deep memory of Hebe which brought each canvas to life, mesmerizing all who looked upon them. Even though Hebe and everything that had transpired was permanently gone from his mind, she was still being remembered through Richard's art. Mercifully, he never had to lament that he was the one who sent her into oblivion.

FRANCIS AND THE SOLDIER
A CIVIL WAR STORY
Ronald Lloyd

As Francis Anna Vaughn Davies, Frannie to the family, came out of her bedroom and into the dogtrot, she felt a tug on her floor-length skirt. Looking back, she saw the hem had snagged. Muttering an un-lady-like curse, she grumbled to herself; *How many times had she asked Logan to do something about that nail?*

Resisting the impulse to rip it free, she balanced Gillie Mertis, her year-old son, in one arm as she lifted the skirt with the other. The Yankie blockade, so laughable a year ago, was beginning to bite. Now, even everyday clothes were becoming precious.

Hearing the hinges of a door squeal, Francis turned. Through the tunnel formed by her bedroom on the right and the parlor and dining room on the left, Francis saw Sarah Jane exit the small kitchen that sat a few yards behind the main house. At the sight of her maid, she felt a surge of relief. *Sarah had not run off during the night.*

All any of her friends or neighbors could talk about these days was how many of their slaves had fled to the Union Army in Memphis. With freedom only a few miles to the West, a steady stream of slaves tramped past their plantation every night.

With a shake of her head, she wondered; *How long would it be before their own slaves fled to the Union lines?*

Coming up the two steps into the dogtrot, the servant saw her mistress and stopped. "Sarah Jane," Francis said, "I left my dirty clothes in my room. See that they're laundered."

Nodding, Sarah replied, "Yes, 'am. Gets to it rights afer breakfast."

Her voice rising, Francis glared at her servant. "You'll get to it now, not in an hour, not in ten minutes, you'll do it now. Do you understand?"

Wincing, Sarah Jane's head bobbed as she said, "Yes, 'am. I's gets to it rights now."

Continuing across to the parlor, Francis frowned; *Tarnation, even the ones who didn't run away were becoming more uppity by the day.*

Once in the parlor, she turned right, passed the stairs to the bedroom they called the Loft, and entered the dining room. Her husband, Logan Early Davies, sat at the far end of the table and in front of the fireplace. Placing Gillie in his highchair, she looked up and said, "Good morning, Mister Davies."

Raising his head from the newspaper he was reading, Logan lifted a napkin to wipe his lips and bushy black beard. "Good morning, Franny. Did you sleep well?"

Once she was sure the baby was secure, Francis moved around the corner of the table and said, "Yes, dear." Satisfied, he returned to the newspaper.

A study in contrasts, their union had raised many an eyebrow in the close-knit farming community of Southwest Tennessee. Francis had only been nineteen when they married two years ago, and he had been nearly forty. But their differences didn't stop there; large and masculine, he towered over her petite frame, his long and angular face so different from her slightly round, soft, and feminine features. The only thing they seemed to have in common was their dark black hair.

Settling into her chair, Francis asked, "Any news?"

Lowering the paper, Logan shook his head. "Not much, and what there is is over a week old."

At his words, she nodded in understanding. When the northern army arrived, the Memphis Daily Appeal had loaded up its presses and, using a series of wagons and rail cars, fled before the advancing Union forces. Since then, it had moved so often, many now called it the Moving Daily Appeal.

Rising, Logan laid the paper beside her plate, saying, "Here, read it yourself. I need to get going. We're working the back forty today."

"Mister Davies, please slow down. You're working yourself to death."

"Someone has to do it, darling. With my brother James in the army, there's no one else."

As Logan came around the table, the back door opened, and Anjaline, the cook, entered with a plate of ham and eggs. Before the servant could lay her breakfast on the table, Francis heard horse's hooves coming up the lane in front of the house.

Hearing the parlor door open, she saw Joshua, their stable hand, enter, his eyes filled with fright. "Masa, Yankies are a comen up the lane."

Turning to his wife, Logan said, "I'll see what they want."

Once her husband was through the door, she jumped up. Entering the parlor, Francis crossed to the front window and peering between the curtains, saw three men coming up the dirt path to the house. As they passed the horse paddock on their right, she saw the one in the middle, a civilian, was wearing a shabby suit. On either side, there were two Union soldiers, one an officer and the other a sergeant.

As the trio approached, her husband stepped to the porch's edge and looking down at them, asked, "What do you want? Haven't you stolen enough already? I can barely feed my people now."

Stopping a few feet from the steps, the shabby man announced in a high-pitched whine, "Now, Mister Davies, don't be like that. We're here to do business with you."

"Business?"

"We want to contract for your cotton."

"I don't do business with invaders."

Seeing the sergeant look her way, Francis moved to the side of the window and could not see who spoke, but she assumed it was the officer. "Sir, first of all, we're not invaders. Tennessee is a part of the United States. Second, what will you do with your cotton if you don't sell to us? We'll just confiscate it, and if we don't confiscate it, the rebels will burn it to keep us from getting it. I don't see that you have much choice."

Moving around so she could peer out with one eye, Francis saw the weaselly man take a paper out of his pocket. "Here's the standard contract. I think you'll see it's very reasonable."

Her husband took the document, scanned it, and tossed it on the ground. "You're only offering me a third of the pre-war price. It's worth triple last year's price in England."

Leaning down to get the paper, the whiny man said, "But how would you get it there, sir?"

Before the civilian could retrieve the paper, the officer said, "Leave it." Turning, he added, "Mister Davies, sign that paper. We'll be back when pickin' time comes."

Stopping mid-turn, the officer studied the horse in the paddock beside the house and said, "Nice mare."

Seated in a rocking chair, Francis sat in the parlor, her needle moving rhythmically. Raising the embroidery, she frowned. *No matter how hard she tried, it never was as good as her mother's.*

Hearing the plop-plop of hooves in the lane, Francis rose and, peering out the window, saw Logan approaching the hitching post at the end of the path to the lane. Dismounting, he tied his horse to the post and turned toward the house. Coming out into the dogtrot, she stepped into the sunlight. "Mister Davies, Is something wrong?"

Waving his hand in negation, Logan turned toward the side of the house. "No. I'm here to get a file from the barn. The hoes are so dull, it takes three whacks to cut a stock."

As Logan disappeared around the house, she returned to her needlework, but about a minute later, she heard more hooves coming up the lane. Rising, she peered out the window and saw it was the officer from this morning.

Unsure what to do, she watched as the man approached the mare, dismounted and began to stroke the horse's nose. Suddenly, his intent was apparent.

Her first impulse was to get her husband, but the barn was more than three hundred yards behind the house. By the time she got to the barn and brought her husband back, the officer and the horse would be long gone.

With a nod, she decided she must act. Turning, she retreated through the parlor and out the back door of the dining room. Crossing the few feet to the kitchen, she entered the side door and saw a large butcher knife lying on the table in the middle of the room. Snatching it up, she whirled and ran toward the house, ignoring Anjaline's questions.

Her long skirts aflutter, she charged through the dogtrot and down the front steps. Once on the path, Francis slowed to a fast walk, concealing the knife in the folds of her skirt as she cried, "May I help you, sir?"

Turning, the officer appeared startled by her unexpected appearance but, seeing it was a woman, did not reply. Reaching down, he began untying the reins as Francis continued down the path. Again, she cried, "Sir, I said, may I help you?"

Irritated, the officer turned and, with a superior smirk, said, "No, I just came for the horse."

Tightening her grip on the knife, she announced, "Sir, that is not your horse; it belongs to my husband."

Returning to his task, the officer said, "Not anymore. It belongs to the United States Army now."

Coming to the end of the path, she took ahold of the bridle with her left hand, the knife handle biting into her right. "Sir, you can't have the horse."

As he released the knot, Francis whipped the blade out. Bringing it up, she brought the knife down, slicing the leather in two. Startled, the officer stood, the ends of the severed reins limp in his hand as Francis pulled the horse away. Looking at the officer, she announced, "I have my horse. Now go."

An Afterword

Let me take my storyteller hat off and become a historian again. As with all family stories, this one has been told and retold, and I am sure, grew with each generation. As I researched the account, one part of the story perplexed me. Growing up on a farm, I am familiar with horses and bridles. I have worked on harness leather and remember how hard it was to cut. Also, the reins would have hung limp between the horse and soldier, making a strike ineffectual.

My suspicions were confirmed when I visited with the Executive Director of the Davies Manor Museum. When I told her about my story, she said, "There was no contemporary evidence of the event."

But I decided to keep it because, like all myths, it tells a greater truth. It reminds us of the strength of character and resilience of these frontier wives and mothers. Frannie, our heroine, lived only a few more years, dying in 1865 at the age of twenty-four (24). Logan never remarried.

SICKENINGLY SWEET
Beth Krewson Carter

I wasn't even looking for a house, not really. Blake had just left, and I was stretched out watching Jimmy Fallon. Out of boredom, I finally got up and moved over to my couch to eat a box of crackers. Sitting in the dark, I scrolled through Zillow until something made me stop. A photo of a candy apple red front door filled the screen. Something about the white painted brick and green shutters whispered to me, nudging my fingers to swipe on every interior shot. By the time I got to the last picture, mist clouded my vision, because I could see the two of us living there, putting Christmas lights around the windows.

We planned to arrive early for the open house. Both of us wanted to check out the neighborhood. I don't know if my ADHD was in full swing, or it was the happy butterfly in my stomach, but

I parked on the curb just as the sun peeked over the roof top. Two couples walking their dogs nodded at me and a man on the corner waved before cutting his grass. Each time someone acknowledged me, a smile edged across my face. Everything was quiet and ordinary yet tinged with an extraordinary sparkle.

I studied the house, memorizing every line and angle, as the sunlight changed the color of the front door to a warm rust. All of a sudden, a little girl turned the handle and ran to the edge of the yard. She looked about seven, and when she climbed onto the swing in the oak tree, my heart gave a little squeeze. The strands of her long hair blew behind her like ribbons of honey. My eyes followed her, unable to look away, as she rose higher in the air. For the first time, I believed in signs. She was my omen, a mirror of the family we would become.

Blake texted, promising to arrive soon, so I sat in the driver's seat as the minutes became an hour. A steady stream of people strolled up the walkway. Every person looked like the type of buyer who knew their credit score and was already preapproved by their bank. What if we weren't ready? But then I remembered that sometimes life happens whether we're ready or not.

After most of the lookers were gone, I opened my car door and straightened my clothes. Blake was nowhere in sight, but it was fine. Running late didn't mean anything. He sometimes failed to show up for things, especially if he got caught up in a meeting with his campaign manager.

As I walked up the driveway, a strange mixture of nerves and excitement made my steps drag on the concrete. I wasn't sure what to expect, but then I opened the door. The air smelled of soy candles and lemons. In the living room, a brick fireplace next to the big window captured my imagination. A longing for a chilly evening tugged at me, until I went into the white kitchen, and the tiny bistro table set for two made me suddenly want to cook breakfast. I don't even remember walking down the hallway, but the lavender bedroom with a unicorn pillow stopped me dead in my tracks. Without meaning to, my hand ran ever so slightly over the wall as I shut my eyes. It was perfect for us, all of us.

Back at the front door, the real estate agent had a bobbed haircut and an almost charming gap in her front teeth. Like most saleswomen, she feigned interest in me, and I let her do most of the talking. I only looked at my phone twice, thinking I had missed a call from Blake, but my screen was dark. After she pressed her card into my palm, I slipped outside and breathed a sigh of relief tinged with yearning.

I got back in my car and calculated mortgage payments. We could do this. Even if I took a few months off, we could make it work.

Before I got carried away, my eyes slid over to the passenger seat. The bag from Cottontails had pink tissue paper stuffed in the top. I tried to imagine Blake's reaction. In my mind, I could already see her. She was going to look exactly like him.

Whenever we talked about next year, Blake always took my hand, promising we would have the whole world. More than once, he even showed me pictures of rings on his phone. I nodded in agreement at all the large settings because he had no idea that I liked simple solitaires. All I wanted was a single stone to tell everyone I was his one and only.

As soon as I pulled away from the curb, my stomach lurched. Even though I hadn't been able to keep things down, the feeling caught me by surprise. I took a sip of Sprite and then an odd mixture of hunger mingled with the sourness rising in my throat. When I turned onto Poplar Avenue, the idea of a bear claw dominated my thoughts.

The parking lot of Gibson's Donuts forced customers to exercise their parking skills as well as their persistence. When a space finally opened, I whipped my hatchback between the lines and pretended I didn't see the old man muttering at me in his SUV. Adjusting my sunglasses, I ignored his stare and made a bee line for the entrance.

An aroma of warm yeast and sugar wrapped around me as I stood in line. Even though I had become super weird about smells, the donuts offset the coffee just enough to make my mouth water. When it was my turn at the counter, I acted like a good, responsible adult and ordered a carton of milk along with my bear claw.

I was in a corner booth, reaching in my purse for a huge beige vitamin, when a large group came through the door. At first, I didn't pay much attention because I assumed they were some sort of celebrity, maybe a Grizzlies player and his entourage. But then I saw him. First, it was the finance director, then the slicked back hair of his campaign manager, and finally there was Blake.

The three of them all had expressions on their faces like they were ready to worship the voters. They made just enough commotion to turn heads. With each wave and handshake, I heard the words "running for governor".

Thanks to my big Anne Klein sunglasses, I had a front row seat. I took a bite of the frosted edge of my bear claw and then sat back to watch. Blake always complained about impromptu public attention, but he looked relaxed, smiling, even as if he enjoyed all the fuss. I was almost proud of the way he handled himself until he turned. He put his arm around her shoulder, and I could feel it. I had the weight of his arm draped around me committed to memory. Before I could flinch, he leaned over and kissed his wife's cheek. She smoothed her hair, her huge cluster of diamonds on her left hand catching the sunlight.

In an instant, the shop was too warm. The room wobbled at the same moment everything fell into perfect focus. The sick feeling roared again in my stomach.

The group laughed in front of the glass display case, so I rose from my seat. No one noticed me which made me glad and furious all at once. Taking my order, I slipped out the door, hating the way I couldn't stop looking at my feet.

When I sat in my car, I thought I might cry. Hadn't Blake noticed the bumper sticker in the parking lot? I had one with his name in big bold letters plastered across my back window. A hollow, numb sensation filled my insides and I cursed myself for caring as I turned the key in the ignition.

Driving was a blur until I gagged and pulled into the Corky's Barbeque parking lot. The smell of pulled pork danced in the breeze. I opened my door and got sick on the pavement. A worker in an apron stopped emptying trash and frowned at me. He put his hands on hips, and I mouthed an apology because he looked mad, like he would have to clean up my mess.

In my glove box, I searched for a napkin to wipe my face, when my hand felt something hard. Pulling out the smooth edge, I was almost surprised to see my old phone. Then I remembered. I put it there after I got soaked in the rain at Memphis is May. Once I got a new one, I forgot all about that day with my girlfriends.

I stared at the black screen, remembering Blake's reaction to my dilemma.

"Just get a new phone and number. And let's not text this time except for quick messages. Until my divorce is final, I don't need a trail of our communications. I'm not worried about my wife, because it's over, but it just doesn't look good for my campaign."

At the time, I agreed. The last thing I wanted was to ruin the career he worked so hard to create.

I cradled the old phone in my hand and my eyes dropped to the pink tissue paper. I was suddenly alone, but I wasn't, not anymore. The future spun out before me, and I knew I needed to be smart before it was too late.

My old charger was still in the console, so I plugged in the phone. A bright screen prodded me. Maybe being in a hot car for a month was the perfect trick, or perhaps fate was offering me an escape. I checked my text messages. They were all there.

"A reporter has been calling my friends and colleagues offering a large amount of money if they have any dirt on me," Blake told me late one night. There was disgust in his voice, and I shook my head in disbelief. How could someone be so awful? I rubbed his back to soothe him.

"Don't worry about people like that," I said.

"Her name is Dawn Waters, and her byline is always about cleaning up politics and exposing candidates and the lies they tell. She's always looking for the next big scoop."

I forced myself to dismiss all the memories and the rising pain in my chest. Holding the phone, I weighed my options. Before I made any final decision, I googled her name. She was easy to find.

My finger hovered over her contact and then it dropped onto her number. A female voice answered on the second ring.

"Dawn Waters."

I shut my eyes; my throat was tight.

"Hello? Is someone there?" she asked.

My hand went to my stomach.

"Yes," I managed to say. "Are you still paying for information about candidates running for governor, namely Blake Livengood?"

"Absolutely, but I do require proof."

A little bit of me was dying, or maybe the last embers of my heart were gasping, but I was already planning. My aunt in North Myrtle Beach was always begging me to help her run her vacation rental business. I would call her and visit, and perhaps stay.

"Yes, I have proof that Blake is not the family man he claims to be. Will that do?"

There was a pause on the line. My heart banged in my chest. What if she wanted more than personal lies, and my text messages weren't enough for her?

"Meet me at the Starbucks in Germantown in thirty minutes. If your information is good, I'll pay you."

The line went dead and for the first time, I could breathe. My sickness was gone, and I was ravenous. I bit into the bear claw with everything I had.

GOOD EEEEVENING FROM NEVER NEVER LAND
Annette Cole Mastron

I park at the northeast corner of Main and Beale, grabbing the white paper sack and my toolbox as I step out of the car. I dodge two trolleys and cross to the majestic Orpheum Theater. I walk down the Beale Street side of the building to the stage door, watching the sun disappear into the Mississippi River. I glance over my shoulder to a Friday night on Beale just getting underway. I see a horse drawn hearse creeping up Beale drawing the attention of the gawking tourist and give a shudder as it draws closer to Main Street. It's being driven by a vampire-clad man complete with a cape. The Sivad wanna-be turns south on Main, disappearing from my view, thankfully.

I knock on the stage door and Abe opens the door and says, "Hey, Miss Teresa, how are you doing?"

"Weird lawyering day, Abe, but I'm happy to be here. I love

keeping the Mighty W in good shape."

The Orpheum's Mighty Wurlitzer Pipe Organ is such a jewel in the crown of this theater. Built in North Tonawanda, New York and installed at the Orpheum in 1928, it was purchased to play for vaudeville shows and silent movies. A true gem, since so few still exist. The summer movie showings and special occasions, like the All Hallow's Ball tomorrow night, require it to have regular maintenance.

"I'm glad Vincent Astor taught me how to do it before he died," I continue. "Hey, I brought you some Gibson's donuts. Here you go." I hand him the white paper bag.

"Oh, thank you, I'll save it for my break and see if Mary-Mary the ghost comes out when I'm eating donuts. She has a sweet tooth, you know."

"You've seen her? So, what's the story of Mary-Mary? I saw where various ghost hunters have tried to root her out, to no avail. I read that the Broadway cast of *Fiddler on the Roof* held a seance on the stage, and she refused to appear."

Abe explains, "Mary-Mary, as in the nursery rhyme, was supposedly killed in a trolley accident at Beale and Main. She is contrary in her appearances. She's a mischievous, twelve year old girl with black shoulder length hair. She's dressed in a glowing old fashioned white dress, with dark stockings and no shoes. Back in the early 1900s shoes were expensive, and people weren't buried with them. I think that's why she doesn't have any on when she's been seen. The song that draws her out is from *Peter Pan*; I can't remember the name of it."

I ask again, "Have you seen her?"

"Of course, but Vincent Astor saw Mary-Mary many times. I miss him but he's at peace now. He was such a moving force to save the Orpheum from the wrecking crew. I better let you get to work."

I turn and go to the orchestra pit and descend to the organ. We hear a pounding on the stage door.

"I'll be back," Abe says, as he ambles toward the door.

The theater turns icy cold like a north wind just blew through from Main Street to Front Street. I open Vincent's toolbox, which is mine now, and start the maintenance checklist taped to the lid. I'm on step #12, the last one on the list. I press the raise button which shudders slightly and begins the assent out of the orchestra pit. I play "Never Never Land" from the musical *Peter Pan* as an homage to Mary-Mary, but suddenly feel very cool, actually frigid. I turn and see Mary-Mary sitting next to me on the bench. She appears to grin as she climbs onto the organ keys and hops to the stage and dances away in the left wing out of sight.

Abe returns and says, "Weird, no one was there."

The words hang in the air, and from the open center lobby door a voice drawls, "Good Eeeevening."

I turn on the organ bench as a shiver runs up my spine. Glowing white in the dark theater, effervescent Mary-Mary hops from a stage wing down the few stage stairs and runs down the center aisle. The man clad as Sivad is there; he was the scary bane of my middle school existence. Now, I'm puzzled. Who is he and why is he here?

"Good Eeeevening, Miss Mary," he says as she dances around him. "I'm here to drive you to the others." He tips his top hat to me and Abe and takes Mary by the hand and walks into the lobby.

I lower the organ into the orchestra pit and run down the center aisle with Abe following. "Sivad" is walking through the entrance of the Orpheum to his waiting horse-drawn hearse. He swings Mary-Mary up to the seat and climbs up to sit next to her.

"But wait!" I shout. "Mary-Mary belongs here at the Orpheum!"

Mary-Mary waves at Abe and me as "Sivad" turns and says, "Miss Teresa, I said good eeeevening." With that, he clicks to the horses and they start to move south on Main Street, as I just stare at them.

Abe comes next to me and says, "Let's go split my donut. I think we need some sugar."

The bag crinkles as he opens it. We sit on the stage, picnic style, and he gives me half of the custard-filled chocolate long-john donut.

Abe asks, "Why were you so creeped out by Sivad?"

"To answer that you'd have to know middle school me. You see, in 7th grade no sleepover was successful unless you could watch WHBQ's Friday night show *Fantastic Features*. It's how I saw all the creepy Vincent Price movies and the Godzilla movies that were originally Japanese but dubbed in English, so the mouths of the actors were off as you watched the movie. 'Sivad', the host of the show, scared us all before the featured horror or sci-fi movie of the week even began. Many of those movies I watched with my hands over my eyes peeking through my fingers like they were Venetian blinds.

"Later I learned that 'Sivad' was created by Watson Davis, the advertising director for the Malco theater that was located at this location before the theater reclaimed its former name, The Orpheum, in the 1980s. Davis created 'Sivad'—his last name spelled backwards—and had the whole vampire costume, complete with a red satin lined black cape, cane, top hat and false vampire teeth. The show began each week with Sivad driving a horse-drawn, beveled glass-sided hearse in a foggy Overton Park near the Brooks Art Gallery. He would stop the hearse, climb down from the driver's seat, and pull a coffin from the back of the hearse. Middle school me didn't think about how one person could do that alone. Then, he would slowly lift the lid and smoke would escape from inside the coffin. It was so creepy.

"All this was done to music of Leigh Stevens' score from the 1950 sci-fi film *Destination Moon*. Sivad, with his vampire teeth close to the camera would say, "Good eeeevening, I am Sivad, your monster of ceremonies." Terrifying to middle school me! You remember Happy Hal's toy store on Union? He even had Sivad Halloween costumes."

Abe finishes his half of the donut and says, "I forgot all about Sivad after Watson Davis died, but I sold records he made as Sivad at my store on Beale back in the day. I think the title was "Sivad Buries Rock & Roll" with "Dickey Drakeller" on its flip side. Do you think the guy who picked up Mary-Mary was the ghost of 'Sivad'? I just thought he was publicity for tomorrow night's party."

I finish my half of the donut and answer, "Geez, like I know. Whoever it was seemed real familiar with our little ghost Mary like he had picked her up before. My tuning checklist is finished. I'm done for tonight. You wanna go follow them?"

Abe locks up, and I retrieve my SUV, picking him up in front of the Orpheum exactly where the horse-drawn hearse had been ten minutes before. I wait on a trolley to pass and head south down Main Street in the direction of the hearse.

"Oh no!" exclaims Abe.

"Is that the hearse in front of Earnestine and Hazel's?" I say. "No way am I going in there; it's dubbed the most haunted bar in America! No, thank you." I pull to the curb and park behind the hearse. Thankfully, the hearse is empty, no coffin in sight.

Abe pats my hand and says, "Did you know the original building was a church back in the late 1800s?"

"So, like it's a sanctuary for vampires and ghosts? Naw, that's for immortals like in The Highlander series. What I know is that I was here on the day James Brown died. I was eating one of their famous Soul burgers and the front jukebox randomly started playing 'I Feel Good'. It kept playing that song over and over until they finally pulled the plug, cutting off electricity to it. Cue the Twilight Zone music. They even give ghost tours here which includes the upstairs that once was once a brothel."

"You know if we don't go in you'll always be curious and wonder," Abe reasons.

"You're right, I do wanna know what's going on. Let's go find Mary and 'Sivad' and a host of hopefully friendly ghosts. I'm hoping for Caspers and not Lucifers."

I look at Abe as we get out of the SUV and say in my best southern drawl 'Sivad' voice, "Good eeeevening. Let's go see if 'Never Never Land' is on the jukebox."

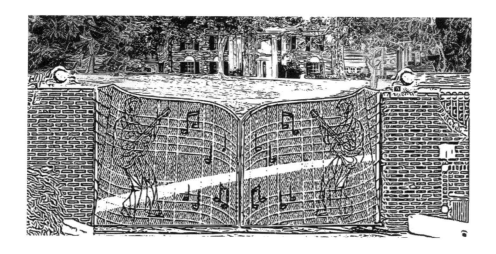

WE WILL ALL BE RECEIVED IN GRACELAND
Judy Creekmore

Mom met Iris in a bus station cafe in Birmingham many years ago, and they wrote to each other sporadically. This led to Iris inviting me to visit after Mom died. It seemed fitting that I arrived in Memphis by bus. As I waited several minutes for my ride I couldn't fail to see all the signs singing the praises of Graceland. Elvis' House! Elvis' Museums! Elvis' Plane! Even the graves of the whole Presley clan!

From a block away I knew that a rube named C was coming for me in a tricked-out 1949 pick-up truck the color of mustard. All the way to Plain Sight, Arkansas he kept telling me how happy he was that Iris was having company. "No charge for the ride," he said. "Iris'got it covered."

I've stayed in some dumps in my time, but the house he stopped in front of was a cross between Dust Bowl-era derelict and cement gnome heaven. It was surrounded on three sides by soybean fields. I gave C my best withering you've-got-to-be-kidding look. He returned it with a big old dimpled grin, his head bobbing. "Yer gonna love it here with Iris."

My hand was barely free of the truck door handle when dust from the spinning wheels flew up my nose and into my eyes. I lifted the bottom of my best t-shirt and wiped my face. Before I could turn and yell, "Hey!" C and his condiment-colored carriage were halfway back to town.

Iris reached out and pulled me in despite my attempt to stay out on the porch just a bit longer. She hugged my neck, patted my back, and shooed something lurking in the shadows of the porch. I made all the polite noises Mom had taught me as I entered the gloom of the house.

"We've fixed up Trini's room for you," she said, including her scrawny cat, Mr. Tuxedo, who wove himself in and out of her steps as she led the way.

Trini's room wasn't what I expected after passing through the cramped living room. To get there we walked over holes—I mean holes, not bare spots—in a dirty, stick-to-the-bottom-of-your-shoes carpet that led down a sun-deprived hall. Don't ask for colors, because whatever colors had been there during the Eisenhower administration were either obliterated by grime, faded by time, or, I suspect, bleached by cat urine. Yeah, the house smelled funny, too.

The window was open in Trini's room and I gave silent thanks for sunlight and fresh air. There was a brass bed with a brightly colored patchwork quilt, a brass and plastic make-up table with a silver-plated vanity set, a new-looking rag rug, and a wooden dresser painted white. Faded posters of David Cassidy served as backdrops for hundreds of magazine photos of the 70s heartthrob. They were thumb-tacked over all the non-David Cassidy-face areas. "Nice," I said, trying not to be freaked by all those teenage eyes leering at me.

"Trini loved David Cassidy, you know," Iris said, smoothing a non-existent wrinkle from the quilt. "I saw him on Ellen recently." She brought her lips to within kissing distance and I almost ran before she whispered, "She's a lesbian from New Orleans, you know."

"Mmm, yeah." I imitated C's big bobble movement and stepped over to the dresser. A David Cassidy bubblegum card sat propped against the mirror.

"That's when he was Keith Partridge. I always liked Keith Partridge and his momma—she raised that family all by herself, except that silly Reuben sometimes helped. I often wondered about their relationship. I reckon he was gay because he never even gave her one lustful look. I never much cared for David Cassidy. I was an Elvis fan."

"Yeah?"

She did her bobblehead move. "Oh, he loved his baby girl, Lisa Marie," she said while fluffing the bed pillows.

"When he's not singing silly songs about clams and gets serious, he has a lot to say. About love. Through the years I've needed to be reminded about love."

With a quick about-face, she waved for me to follow. "Make yourself at home, then come on out to the kitchen. You saw the bathroom? I'll have dinner on the table by the time you wash up."

I washed the dust off as best I could while taking stock of the scum and mold in the small bathroom. I tried not to touch anything as I followed my nose to the kitchen on the far side of the house. I prayed that the smell was an overflowed septic tank or an upwind paper mill. Once or twice I thought of turning back, getting my suitcase, and hoofing the five or six miles to town. Maybe try to hitch a ride. Maybe catch the next bus going anywhere. Seemed like a lot of work.

Iris lifted the lid on a huge pot and the stink poured into the room—a moist, suffocating odor that would have brought my stomach contents to the surface if I'd eaten within the past 24 hours. They say that you can eat anything if you're hungry enough. That's a lie.

"Mr. Tuxedo has been waiting patiently." Iris bent and scratched the inside of the cat's ragged ear and checked her finger. "Mites. They come and go." Mr. Tuxedo shook his head.

I'm here because I have nowhere else to go. The chant first popped into my head during the bumpy truck ride with C.

"Since we don't often have guests for dinner, Mr. Tuxedo and I thought we'd share one of our favorite meals. Turkey necks and mustard greens!"

I may have turned green. I know I sat down hard on a metal and plastic chair that had been repaired several times with duct tape.

Iris stopped mid-transfer of steaming slime from pot to plate. "Those long bus rides will do it to you every time. Let me get you a little co-cola to settle your stomach before we eat."

"Crackers?" I begged. "Open a window?"

After assuring Iris that I would be fine with commodity cheese, crackers, and a generic soda, I encouraged her to fill her own and

Mr. Tuxedo's plates from the simmering pot.

"It's been a long time since we've had an overnight guest. Mr. Tuxedo was just a kitty the last time." After a liberal salt and peppering with an Elvis and Priscilla shaker set, Iris picked up a still steaming turkey neck. Even with her big old teeth, she effortlessly gnawed the good from between the tiny bones of several necks. "In your momma's letters, she said she liked it real well at the nursing home. I'm sorry The Lord called her home so soon."

With the dissipating smell of turkey necks, a little solid food in my stomach, and a slow, steady serenade of purring around my ankles, I began to feel more agreeable, and talkative.

"Yeah. Putting her in the facility was a tough decision to make, but with my bad back, I wasn't much good to either of us."

"She said you hurt your back."

"Just enough to mess me up."

"I got a touch of the arthritis myself." Iris held up her hands and I could see fingers that showed more than a touch of arthritis. "The doctor says that keeping my hands busy helps keep them limber, but it's getting harder to use them. I don't need a lot to live on, but if I can't use my hands, I can't make and sell tea cakes. That's how we pay for our little luxuries."

"Like these turkey necks?"

Iris nodded.

"Like paying C for my ride?"

"A bag of tea cakes don't come near paying for the gas it takes him to come from town. C's just good-hearted, and it's my little way of thanking him."

"You must make good tea cakes if people buy them." I looked around and saw that cat hair covered most of the kitchen counter and assumed the one clean spot must be where she made the cookies.

"My four-times great grandma's recipe. The VFW wants 15 dozen for their next big meeting."

We must have both been thinking for a while about how we could work something out to our mutual benefit. I started to speak, but Iris beat me to it. "When your momma wrote and said you needed someplace to stay, I got to admit that I thought maybe you could come here and I could give you room and board. You could help me with my tea cakes, and whatever little check you get for disability."

I'd like to say that what came out was a polite sigh, but I suspect it was more of a snort. "And when you said I could come, I was thinking how I could help you out and you could pay me a little something." I ran my finger around a damp circle left on the tabletop by the sweating soda can to help me think about what to say next. "Right now I'm between the cracks, but I do expect to draw something one of these days, then I'd be glad to help you with money. Until then, maybe I can work out my room and board, like helping with the tea cakes, maybe some light housework?"

Iris scratched at what looked like a bit of dried egg just beyond her plate, scooped it up on a thick, yellow fingernail, and handed the morsel down to Mr. Tuxedo.

"You can take down those posters if you want to. I don't think Trini'd mind. I buried her with her favorite David Cassidy edition of Tiger Beat magazine. Law, it's been nearly 35 years now."

I followed Iris to the stove and held my breath while we emptied the pot of boiled turkey necks and put leftovers in the refrigerator.

"We're going to get along fine." Iris put the pot into a sink of soapy water. Before I could find a dishcloth to start washing it, she motioned for me to follow her. "You like Oprah?"

I studied the stove top covered with old boil-overs and food spatters so thick they'd make a complete meal for Mr. Tuxedo and left the kitchen without comment. I nearly tripped over him and noticed that cat hair fanned out from the bottom of my shoes as we walked down the hall. More cat hair floated around before resettling on the nasty carpet.

I considered the $27 left from Mom's final check. Most of it was stuffed in my bra.

Iris fumbled with the television remote control. "Oh good, this is the one where Oprah has all the Elvis impersonators! See how young she looked then? It was before she started trying all those weight-loss programs."

She waved toward the sofa, afraid to take her eyes off Oprah, lest she miss something important. She spent a lot of effort lowering herself into a cat-clawed recliner and tucking in a lap quilt featuring Elvis caressing a microphone.

The sofa had been likewise shredded by Mr. Tuxedo, or maybe some long-forgotten cat that was probably buried in the backyard. Cotton stuck out from between strips of duct tape on the arms, and foam bulged from holes in the cushions. One of the cushions was pretty much threadbare, but still fully covered.

Settling into somebody else's butt imprint, I made myself comfortable on the sofa.

Yeah, I decided, *I could get used to this.*

It took a couple of days to get my bearings. I learned that there was a radio station that played nothing but Elvis and that Iris had the radio in the kitchen tuned to it. I began to notice details like a graphic of swivel-hipped Elvis on a plate, or a World's Best Mom plaque under the grime and cat hair.

I had collected Iris's cleaning rags and products and put them to work. "So that's Elvis and Priscilla?" I realized after washing a plastic cutting board.

All the while she cautioned me not to over-do. I realized by "over-do" she meant for me to stay out of her stuffed-to-capacity bedroom. Like Trini's shrine to David Cassidy, Iris had many magazine photos, album covers, and one signed photo of The King. She did not want the newspapers, yellow and brittle with age to be moved, or her Graceland bedspread to fade in the wash.

We spent the next couple of weeks learning about each other. I didn't tell her about my run-in with an Atlantic City loan shark, and I suspected she had some things she didn't want me to know about.

Within the year I'd begun to collect Social Security benefits. Between us, we had enough money to have her old car repaired and even buy gas once in a while. Our monthly outings were to West Memphis for grocery shopping and to a fast-food restaurant.

A couple of years passed when one day, Iris was hanging laundry outside and someone from her bank called and assumed I was her. The voice began promoting a new CD rate for her $2 million! All this time, she had been scraping by on her Social Security and interest. I told them I'd call back.

I met her on the back steps, arms akimbo and lips pursed, ready to call her out. "You have more than $2 million in the bank?"

She set the laundry basket down, then didn't know what to do with her gnarled and roughened red hands.

How long will those fingers be able to work a clothespin? I took her hands in mine and we sat on the edge of the porch.

"What are you saving your money for, Iris?"

"My sweet angel, Trini, and dying on the job were the only good things my late husband gave me," she finally said.

"But, why are you saving it? You have enough money in that bank to keep you and Mr. Tuxedo in turkey necks if you both live to be a thousand years old!"

"I might need it someday."

Looking around, I spread my arms wide and did a slow survey of the puddle over the septic tank, rotting porch planks, and other areas where even $1,000 would make a huge difference.

"Why bother fixing up this old place?" she said. "When I'm gone it will either be gutted or pulled down."

"Iris, Trini would want you to spend the money to make your life easier or even just to have some fun."

Iris having an estate is something that had not occurred to me. The idea of it caused the sudden fog in my brain to swirl like a tornado. We sat quiet for a while.

"What is the one thing you keep telling me you dream about doing?"

She had been thinking about it, too. Head still bowed, she whispered, "Visit Graceland."

"I don't know how many times I've heard you say that. Let's go!" I jumped up, ready to get the car keys. "I'm rolling in SS money and you've got a whole bank full. You could visit Graceland, get the deluxe private VIP tour, and buy out their whole gift shop with the money you have."

"One souvenir would be nice to remember it by."

I reclaimed her chapped hands. "Come on, Iris. Let's go!"

She gave me that big old horsey grin and nodded. "Can we invite C? He's always been so good to me." She leaned in, bringing her lips close, and whispered, "He was my husband's son—with a neighbor down the road." She straightened up and her eyes met mine. "I don't bear her any ill will. She shared C with me."

That took a minute to digest, but since C had to be nearly as old as I, it couldn't make much difference now. "Sounds great to me. When he brought me here, he said he's always wanted to go.

"Let's go next week," I suggested.

"No," she said. "Elvis and I will both be 90 in January. Let's go then."

"It'll be cold and crowded."

"But, I'll be wearing a new coat. I have to look nice for Graceland."

And that's how Iris and I met, became friends, and went to Graceland.

Except, Iris died of a heart attack the November before our big trip. I had been outside, setting a couple of new garden gnomes upright after a massive beast of a dog chased Mr. Tuxedo through the yard. When I came in and asked Iris if she'd like a cup of tea, she didn't answer. At first, I thought she was just entranced by the same Oprah rerun that was shown the day I arrived in Plain Sight. I touched her shoulder and her body slumped sideways. I tucked her favorite Graceland throw pillow beneath her head while a Korean Elvis crooned "Love Me Tender."

Early on a rainy January 8, C and I arrived at the Meditation Garden at Graceland. Iris was there, too, wearing her first new coat in many years. I guarded some of her remains in a plastic baggy until it was time to introduce her to Elvis. C stood watch as I pretended to tie my shoelace. The baggy opened easily and I did my best to fling the ashes toward the foot of Elvis' gravestone.

After a few words of good-bye, C leaned over the fence and placed a small bouquet of silk Irises and a bag of tea cakes at the foot of the grave.

If the spirits of Elvis and Lisa Marie, and all the others, roam the grounds of Graceland, I hope they welcomed Iris with open arms and enjoy sharing stories of their favorite cats, gardening tips, and episodes of Oprah.

THE WOMAN IN THE TREES
Deborah Sprinkle

It wasn't until her husband Samuel passed away that Mary Louise Albers realized her true calling. She made the discovery as she went through Sam's belongings. After she emptied a closet or a drawer, Mary Louise gave the space a thorough cleaning.

Pretty soon, she found herself dusting, mopping, and scrubbing the entire house. She hadn't felt so good in a long time, and wished she hadn't let Sam talk her into getting a housekeeper all those years ago.

When Sam became a vice president at his firm, he insisted they hire someone. He said he was only thinking about her. With a housekeeper, she would be free to help at the children's school and volunteer at church.

But that wasn't the real reason.

"Mary Louise, I am a senior executive," he'd said. "We have an image to maintain."

And, as usual, she'd agreed. She loved her husband, and she missed him, but now that he was gone and their children were grown, she decided to fire the housekeeper and clean her own house. Quite simply, she enjoyed it.

One day she had a crazy idea. Why not clean other people's houses as well? She plopped into a kitchen chair, her heart pounding at the thought. Poor Sam. If he weren't dead already, he'd keel over.

It wasn't like she needed the money. Sam left her very comfortable. But the idea of spending the rest of her life going to grandchildren's performances, club meetings, and lunches with friends left her depressed. She needed something to do that made her feel useful.

But was starting her own business the solution? There was only one way she knew to find direction. She settled into her favorite chair and picked up her Bible. After a while, she got to her feet. "I'm going to open my own cleaning business."

She picked up her phone and called Becky Waters, the best friend she had in the world.

"Have you lost your mind?"

That was one thing she loved about Becky, she didn't mince words.

"Let me remind you Mary Louise, you've never run a business before. In fact, except for one summer as a cashier at a department store, you've never worked. And you're old."

"You sound like my girls. Susan said she's worried about my health, that I'm fragile, and Katherine said how can I imagine running a business when I need help handling my own finances." Mary Louise marveled at how calm she felt. Her friend's words only made her more resolute. "I'm not old. I'm middle-aged."

"Okay. Middle-aged."

"I want to do something with whatever time I have left. I want to feel productive."

"But you are productive. You do make a difference." Becky's voice softened. "You're a member of the historic society and you're the head of the book club at the library. Those things are important. And you lead Bible study at church. If that's not worthwhile, I don't know what is."

"I know." Mary Louise sighed. How could she explain the feeling she had to her friend so she'd understand? "This is different. All those things are important, but I do those for others. I would be doing this for me, and I've never done anything just for me before."

Silence crackled across the line.

"I don't completely understand," Becky said. "But I love you and I'll do what I can to help."

"Thank you, sweet friend." Relief flowed through Mary Louise. "I'm going to be very selective about the clients I accept, and I only plan on dedicating two days a week to cleaning to begin with."

"Okay." Becky chuckled. "Then you should name it Elite

Cleaners."

"That's not a bad idea." Mary Louise wrote the words in elegant script on her notepad and smiled.

Within a month, Elite Cleaners was a licensed business with two houses lined up that fit her requirements and her life settled down into a peaceful rhythm. Until one day when she received a call from the elderly lady she cleaned for on Thursday.

"Mary Louise?" she said in her genteel voice. "I'm afraid I have sad news. I won't be needing your help any longer."

"I'm so sorry." A pang of alarm hit Mary Louise. "Did I do something wrong?"

"No. You are a wonderful housekeeper." The woman's voice sounded clogged with emotion. "My daughter and her husband are insisting I move in with them, and my grandson will be living in my house until it's sold."

When her second client called cancelling her service—her daughter lost her job and asked to clean her parents' house for money—Mary Louise wondered if Elite Cleaners was such a good idea after all. Now she was faced with vetting two new people.

Her phone rang a third time, and if Becky's face hadn't appeared on the screen, she wouldn't have answered.

"Hey." Mary Louise sighed.

"I'd say you sound like you lost your best friend, but I am your best friend." Becky's sunny voice sounded through the speaker.

"Very funny." But she couldn't keep the corners of her mouth from turning up in a grin. Another thing she loved about Becky. She always had a way of making her laugh. "I just lost both of my cleaning clients in the last half hour."

"Well then. It's a good thing I called."

"No. I know how you live, and I refuse to clean your house."

"My house is fine. Thank you very much. I don't need your services." Becky paused. "But Davies Manor Historic Site is looking for a cleaning service."

"Are you sure?" Something stirred within her. "How do you know?"

"You haven't been reading the emails from the Historic

Society. They put an ad out."

Mary Louise opened her computer and clicked on Mail. There it was.

"Mary Louise? Are you still there?"

"Yes, sorry. I was reading the ad." It was just like Becky said. A smile slowly spread across her face. "I need to go."

"I figured you would." She chuckled. "Keep me posted."

"I will." Mary Louise pressed End, pulled a notepad over, and jotted down the contact information from the email.

Next, she called her former clients back and asked if they'd be willing to give her references. Which they both said they would. Sterling references. Only one thing left to do. She went to her favorite chair in the family room and picked up her Bible. Time to pray.

Once again, Mary Louise felt that stirring in her spirit, and she knew this was the job for her. She dialed the number from the ad.

"Davies Manor Historic Site. How can I help you?"

"I'd like to speak to someone about the housekeeping position." She'd managed to keep the shaking from her voice. This was just another job, but for some reason, she wanted this one more than anything she'd wanted in a long time.

"Let me transfer you to Mr. Lloyd."

A click and then the warm tones of a male voice sounded on the line. "Frank Lloyd here."

"Mr. Lloyd, I'm Mary Louise Albers, owner of Elite Cleaners, and I'd like to apply for the housekeeping position at Davies Manor."

"Great. Are you available for an interview tomorrow afternoon at five?"

"I'll see you then." Mary Louise pressed End and let out a whoop. She couldn't wait to tell Becky the good news.

≪

It was a rare summer day—not too hot with puffy white clouds hanging in a clear blue sky. Mary Louise pulled next to the silver sedan at the wrought iron gates to Davies Manor. A slim man with silvery hair got out and came over to her window.

"Thanks for coming here to meet me, Mrs. Albers." He extended his hand. "I'm Mr. Lloyd. I'll open the gate. Please follow me to the house."

The tires on Mary Louise's car crunched on the white stone drive that led to the manor house. Stately old oak trees lined the drive.

Déjà vu smacked her between the eyes, and she slowed. Why did it seem so familiar? Mary Louise had never been here before. She touched the silver cross at her neck.

Mr. Lloyd hurried over to open her door. "I thought you might like to see what you'd be getting yourself into."

His easy smile and warm dark eyes eased some of her anxiety. Maybe this wouldn't be so difficult after all. "That was thoughtful of you." She smiled at him.

He led her on a brief tour through the house, starting in the foyer. "This was once an open dogtrot. Do you know what a dogtrot is?"

"Yes. I'm interested in history and belong to the local historical society." She gazed around at all the wonderful antiques. "All these years and I've never visited here before."

"It's pretty fascinating. Let's start in the oldest part of the house, the original one room log cabin." He led her through a door on her left. "As you can see, it's now set up as a sitting room. We have a mixture of reproductions and original pieces. How would you handle cleaning in here?"

"First of all, I'll wear white cotton gloves. I'll use the modern equivalent of a feather duster made from microfibers for the more delicate pieces, and a microfiber dust mop on the wood floor." She looked at the rug. "As for the rug, I'll use a good vacuum on a low setting with an attachment that doesn't have a brush in it."

"Excellent." He beamed at her. "Let's visit the master bedroom next."

The size of the room surprised her. It was as big as the sitting room and contained a four-poster bed, a large chifforobe, washstand, cradle, and a fireplace with a spinning wheel and chair in front of it. Mr. Lloyd had explained that the windows were north and south facing to catch the breezes.

Mary Louise walked to the south window by the bed and gazed out at the expanse of front lawn dotted with towering oaks. A woman in a long dress stood in the shadow of a huge tree to the right of the porch. She was staring at the house. "Mr. Lloyd, are the grounds closed for the night?"

"Yes. Why?"

"There's a woman out there. By that tree." Mary Louise pointed out the window.

Frank Lloyd pulled out his phone. "No one should be here. I'll call security."

Mary Louise glanced at him. When she looked back, the woman wasn't there. "She's gone."

"Did you see where she went?"

"No." Mary Louise placed a hand on her stomach. Her heart pounded in her chest. The woman wasn't staring at the house. She was staring at Mary Louise.

He pressed End. "If she's hiding, they'll find her." He took her arm. "Are you all right?"

"Yes, I'm fine." She gave him a brief smile. "Shall we continue our tour?"

After they'd finished, Mr. Lloyd led her outside to the porch. "What do you think? Are you interested?"

Mary Louise stared at him. "Are you offering me the job?"

"If you want it. I did research on you and liked what I found."

"I'd love to work here." Her smile split her face from ear to ear. "When do you want me to start?"

"Is tomorrow too soon? We'll pay your hourly rate and we would need you to come around five after the museum closes. I'll let you in tomorrow and give you a card so you can get in the gate on your own."

"I'll be here."

"You could do half of the manor one evening and the other half a couple of days later. If that fits into your schedule. This type of cleaning can be very time consuming."

"Perfect. I'm used to working on Tuesdays and Thursdays." Mary Louise refrained from hugging her new boss and simply offered her hand.

"I'll have the contract ready tomorrow for your signature," Mr. Lloyd said.

She called Becky who answered on the first ring.

"Did you get it?"

"Yes." Mary Louise let out all the joy that rose up in her. "Hallelujah! Are you free for dinner?"

"Are you buying?"

Mary Louise laughed.

At five the next day, Mary Louise met Mr. Lloyd at the gate ready to work. "How would you like this done? The downstairs one day and upstairs the next or …?"

"Since the west side of the house includes the dining room and kitchen, let's make that one day," he said. "And the east side plus upstairs the other."

"Very good." Mary Louise stood in the foyer glancing left and right. "I'll start with the west side first, if that's all right with you."

"Fine. I'll be on the back porch working on an exhibit."

Mary Louise entered the sitting room and took out her duster. She worked her way methodically around the room counter-clockwise leaving the large piano for last. The history in the room overwhelmed her. People's needs haven't changed and the ingenuity with which they met those needs never ceased to amaze her.

When she got to the plantation desk, she paused to read the ledger laying open on top. She deciphered the notations and realized it was a pay sheet for workers. At the top of the list were the farm hands. Then indentured servants. Then household help. Her gaze froze on household help, and she gasped.

One of the names listed was Mary Louise Nelson. She was a

housekeeper's assistant. After her name was the notation "Disappeared Nov. 12th, 1867".

Mary Louise steadied herself on the reproduction Victorian settee. Nelson was her maiden name, and November twelfth, her birthday. Movement caught her eye, and she looked out the window. The woman stood once more in the shadow of the oak.

A cry escaped her before she could stop it. What was going on?

Frank Lloyd rushed into the room. "Are you okay?"

"I'm fine." She brushed a hand across her forehead. "A mouse startled me."

"Unfortunately, we can't keep the little vermin out. I'll put another trap in the corner." He surveyed the room. "Looks like you're making excellent progress."

"Yes." The corners of her mouth lifted in a satisfied smile. "I'm almost finished with this room."

"I'll leave you to it."

Mary Louise determined to put the mysterious woman in the trees out of her mind and concentrate on cleaning. Joy filled her heart as she moved from room to room doing the job she loved. After three hours, she stepped onto the enclosed back porch to tell Mr. Lloyd she was through for the day.

"Great. You may be by yourself on Thursday. Will you be okay with that?" He stood and walked with her to the front door.

"Of course." She hesitated. Should she ask him about the journal entry? "I noticed as I was dusting the plantation desk, that there was a housekeeper here in 1867 named Mary Louise Nelson."

"Really?" He cocked his head at her. "How interesting."

She nodded. "My maiden name was Nelson."

"Now that is amazing. Let me see if I can discover anything about her."

"Thank you." Mary Louise glanced at the venerable oak tree where she'd seen the woman. Something stirred once more in her spirit.

Two days later, Mary Louise used the card she'd gotten from Mr. Lloyd to open the gate and the code to enter the house. This time, she started in the main bedroom on the east side of the house.

When she finished, she walked into the porch to leave a note for Mr. Lloyd. An envelope addressed to her lay on the table.

Dear Mrs. Albers,

I discovered something interesting about your namesake from 1867, Mary Louise Nelson. The official story was she walked out on November 12th never to be seen again, but the gossip offered a different one entirely. Rumor had it that Mary Louise was pushed off the balcony, died, and was buried somewhere on the property.

Who killed her and why is unknown. But, according to talk amongst the servants, the owner at the time had her buried and the disappearance story circulated to avoid scandal.

I'm afraid that is as much as I was able to find.
Sincerely,
Frank Lloyd

Mary Louise placed the letter in her purse. As she left, a rumble of thunder rolled across the sky. She crossed the lawn to the big oak tree. Could the woman in the dress be the housekeeper from long ago? Mary Louise skirted the base of the tree examining the roots and bark. Could this be her final resting place?

She placed a hand on the trunk. Nothing. What had she expected? To feel a heartbeat? A jolt of recognition? She turned and touched her cross. Time to go home and eat dinner.

Mary Louise was almost to her car when lightning flashed out of the sky. An explosion sounded so close she dropped to the ground and covered her head. Shrapnel rained down on everything including her and her car.

Wood chips blanketed the ground. She raised her head. The two-hundred-year-old oak tree was cleaved in two all the way to the ground. Luckily, the manor home wasn't damaged.

With shaky fingers, Mary Louise dialed the number for Mr. Lloyd. When he answered, she explained what happened.

"I'll be there in twenty minutes."

Mary Louise put her purse and supplies in her car and picked her way back to the tree. The far side lay open like a gaping wound.

As she drew closer, she noticed something odd. The tree had grown around a large rock, and on the side of that rock someone had carved RIP and the initials MLN. Her heart raced and she lifted her gaze.

The woman in the dress stood ten feet away. She raised her hand in a farewell gesture before fading away. Mary Louise gave a little wave as a sense of peace flowed through her.

GROUP PHOTO ON A BRIDGE
John Burgette

"I think she just wanted a group photo on a bridge," I repeated a little louder.

At that moment, my wife returned from the other room. She stopped abruptly and frowned — there was a long silence except for the early spring sounds of sparrows singing outside the window. We had invited the new couple from next door for a light lunch. They were newlyweds, and they had merely asked about where our wedding had been held.

"So, you're telling that story again, huh? ... Go ahead ..." she said, as she sat down on the green and purple patterned chair. Suppressing a smile, she added, "He always tells it a little differently, so this should be interesting."

She was correct about a different tale with each telling. Many of the details are still patches of a jumbled, jungle fog in my memory — the reason should soon be apparent. So, I often have to guess at the details and creatively surmise what might have really happened.

∽

To just be clear, I wanted to elope. I don't do well with crowds. Just the thought of public speaking causes me to feel dizzy and to break out into a cold sweat. My body becomes rigid as I can feel the multitude of eyes glaring at me. As the groom in a wedding, it was logical to assume that many people would be staring in my direction.

In contrast, my bride was excited and wanted a bigger wedding. When I argued that we didn't have the funds, she brought in her father, who was more than happy to meet her request. It's tradition, right?

Moreover, she had already chosen a location that hosted weddings. There were many other, possible places we could have chosen, but she was most enthusiastic about having the wedding near their Japanese bridge. She wanted to have a group photo of the wedding party on that bridge. She even planned the colors for the suits and gowns — they would complement the red, purple, green, and other hues, which she anticipated would be at the bridge location. I countered that we might just be able to schedule a photo shoot, but no, that would be too much trouble. Besides, the wedding party would already be there for the occasion.

I suppose there's nothing odd about the stress we were experiencing in planning the many steps for the wedding, but we implemented each task like any other complex project. Working with our parents, we were very active in selecting the different services and personnel. My bride's mother had a friend-of-a-friend who agreed to officiate the wedding.

Obviously, a photographer was critical for this event. Our close friend, Gary, was very interested in photography. Beyond just a serious hobby, he occasionally did gigs at parties and events. He assured me that he'd never had any problems during these jobs. Familiar with Gary's work, my bride was delighted and assumed Gary might better capture memorable moments because he knew us well. Gary said he would work directly with the hosts in planning the setup — so, that would be one item we could forget.

He'd never taken photos for a wedding, and when I asked if he was sure he could handle such an event alone, he said, "Of course. Like, what could go wrong?"

I pushed back with a different tactic, "You know, I don't think I'm very photogenic ... and my teeth are awfully stained and crooked."

He chuckled and said, "Oh, don't worry. I can touch-up all that stuff afterwards."

The day of the wedding — for much of the time — is a general blur for me. I do remember a pervading mood of terror. The bride and I had agreed to not see nor talk to each other during the day until the actual event, which was 5:00 PM — we heard it was *bad luck* to do that. So, I probably spent a lot of time ruminating about what might go wrong.

Somehow, I had missed breakfast. I don't remember lunch, either. Other than a small bag of chocolate cookies, I don't remember eating anything. I carried a bottle of water with me, but by late afternoon, I think it was still half full.

When I first arrived at the venue, I recall people helping me with my tie, my coat buttons, my hair, and my shoelaces. I remember it as a confusing dream. Apparently, I must have haphazardly threw on my clothes. I was relieved that some guests weren't afraid to correct my mistakes.

I ran my fingers under my collar and tie. It already felt damp. It's usually hot and humid in July, but it felt very tropical on that day. I remember hearing people complain about record high temperatures. The ceremony was outside, and near the beginning, I surveyed the crowd sitting in the many rows of seats. Many of them were rapidly fanning their faces with a small piece of paper: the wedding program. I overheard someone mutter — thinking I was out of hearing range, I guess — "Why didn't they just elope?"

The memory fog gets very dense at this point, smothered inside that colorful jungle. I recollect the many sweet scents of summer in the air. Looking beyond the crowd I could see dozens of green bushes, multicolor flowers, and singing birds — all under a blue, cloudless sky. At that moment, I wished I could just explore and get lost out there.

As the wedding began, my attention returned to the bride, who looked great. She seemed relaxed and comfortable, yet focused. As she moved next to me — she frowned for a second — I think she whispered, "Are you OK?"

I nodded and smiled bravely. I rose my shoulders, standing very straight and *tall*. I tried to breathe deep and slowly while thinking about the gentle sounds of water flowing across polished rocks.

For me, the ceremony seemed to flow into slow motion. What appeared to be delaying the ceremony was a *lighting of candles*. Although there was an immense dome of heat over us, a strong breeze had suddenly appeared. According to plan, each of our parents was to walk up with a lit wick and then light some ceremonial candles at the front of the procession. Over several minutes, the wind kept blowing too hard — either blasting a wick or extinguishing a ceremonial candle. This episode just kept repeating. Like the needle on a broken record, it skipped back about 30 seconds in a song — over and over.

Finally, I heard someone far in the back hiss, "Can we just pretend they're lit and move on?"

I turned my head, which only made me feel dizzier and nauseous. I think I noticed a couple of glares, but nobody protested as the ceremony continued.

The wedding official seemed to ramble on forever. In fairness, I think I was also losing my sense of time. To calm my anxiety, I tried to concentrate on a small, purple flower petal that had landed on the official's shoulder. I just focused on standing up, very straight — as well as concentrating on that flower petal — trying to appear confident and in control.

There was another strong gust of wind. I watched as the flower petal floated away into the distance. I thought I heard a question — then a long silence — the question was repeated. I didn't understand the question. I considered asking for it to be repeated, but all that emerged from my lips was "Aaahhh ..." The world spun around-round-and-round-up-and-down, while many colors swirled outside the blue sky. Then, I felt my chin hit something very hard.

I remember walking among many colorful flowers of white, red, and purple. I was surrounded by them and their sweet scents. There was the sound of many birds singing a little too loudly. The chirping echoed up and down — then, left to right. I could hear many people talking in different tones and speeds. It reminded me of a chorus singing in some experimental, contemporary jazz style. I guess, maybe, I was dreaming.

I forced my eyes open. I was sitting on a folding chair. There were several people shuffling about me, while some loud, booming voice said, "Back up …. Give him air."

Between those standing near me, I could see guests still sitting in their seats, while they frantically waved their improvised fans. The roaring voice said, "You'll be OK."

I looked up toward the source of the voice. My eyes must have been blurry because I remember seeing shapes and colors — mostly purple and yellow — of a lotus flower. I blinked and saw what I believe was the face of a big fireman — or some type of officer — dressed in a uniform. I thought, *where did he come from?* He added, "It looks like you smashed your face into a rock or something — I think you might have chipped a tooth, too."

He asked when I had last had something to drink. I shrugged as I looked to the left, then to the right. He handed me a bottle of water, and only then did I realize that there was something stuck in my mouth. He gently removed a large piece of blood soaked fabric from my mouth so I could sip on the water. Looking down, I noticed my shirt had several blood spots — I'm not sure what had happened to my jacket, but I realized the fabric that had been in my mouth was my tie. I silently looked back up at him.

"Just to play it safe, I think you should go to the emergency room," he whispered loudly.

A guest, who I didn't recognize, yelled, "What about the wedding?"

The wedding official's face blushed — somewhat like the color of a Japanese maple leaf. He said that there wasn't much more he really had to do, and he could speed things up a bit to finish. In short, we finished exchanging our vows. The bride stood next to me while I sat in the folding chair among a patch of colorful hosta plants.

Once the vows were finished, Gary took a few, quick photos — I was still sitting in the folding chair. Then Gary and my wife helped me up, and they began to escort me to my car. I was oblivious to the crowd — oddly, no longer anxious — until I heard someone say, "What … is that it … is it over?"

Several guests wandered along with us to the parking area. As I sat in the passenger side, my new father-in-law offered to drive us, but my wife said he needed to coordinate the reception. Without asking, Gary hopped into the backseat. My wife started the car. As she looked sadly back toward the direction of the Japanese bridge, she began the drive to the hospital.

I'm not sure how many people it takes to tend a busted mouth. My guess is that our tale began to be repeated not long after we arrived at the hospital, and assorted people kept appearing to offer condolences or ask for more details. Either my wife or Gary would patiently summarize the story. I wasn't always in a position to talk, but anyway, I was too embarrassed to discuss it. A few times, we'd overhear someone else mentioning the incident, and Gary was sure to correct them when they exaggerated or got the facts wrong.

We sat where there were no windows, and it seemed very dark without much color. There was the constant background noise of many people talking, which was frequently interrupted by announcements over the intercom. Occasionally, I'd close my eyes, slowly open them, and I would momentarily see the purple, pink, green, and yellow colors of garden flowers flash across the white walls. Rather than feeling concerned about this discovery, I found it to be a relaxing way to pass the time.

Eventually, a doctor and nurse appeared and began asking us

questions — trying to determine what had happened. They seemed to narrow down the causes as they asked me about how much I had eaten that day or how much water I had consumed. Each time I answered, they both glanced at each other and nodded their heads.

The nurse looked intensely at us and asked, "Did he have his knees locked?"

"Yeah … yeah, I'm sure he did," my wife responded, while Gary displayed a few digital photos of me, taken not long before the collapse. The nurse and doctor looked at each other and nodded their heads.

"That could do it," the nurse stated, satisfied the mystery had likely been solved.

As the medical team was walking away, a random person handed me a half package of stale crackers and said, "Here, this will make you feel better."

Meanwhile, Gary kept trying to take photos of us. Every few minutes, someone from the hospital staff would say something like, "Hey, you can't do that in here!" Gary would explain that it was our wedding day, and the story would once again be rehashed.

As we continued to wait, Gary began showing us photos and videos from his smartphone. Apparently, he had texted his cousin to take photos from the reception. The cousin didn't have a sophisticated camera, but was using his smartphone, and he also liked to take selfies. Every photo was a selfie of Gary's cousin with something from the reception in the background. He sent a few videos of speeches, too. I think one video was of my mom and my father-in-law dancing to some blues music. I'm not sure. Just like the photos, his cousin always had his head in the foreground.

"At least it looks like the reception is going well," Gary said, as he closely studied the images on his phone. My wife and I both looked at each other, nodded our heads, smiled, and began to laugh for the first time we'd been in the emergency room.

After several hours, it appeared they were going to let us leave. We figured we'd still go to the hotel — we had reservations — but we were trying to decide what to do about Gary. As we were finalizing paperwork, I noticed Gary frantically talking to the doctor and a few other, miscellaneous people — a sample of those who had come to hear our story. Occasionally, one of them would look over at us and smile. Gary had talked them into participating in a group photo.

As we were heading toward the exit, we were led onto something like a balcony overlooking an atrium. The railing seemed to be made of some antique wood, and it appeared to be supported by — what looked to me — bamboo poles. Below, I saw Gary aiming his camera at me. My wife and I stood in the middle of the small group. I suppose the doctor was playing the role of the bride's father, while a few other people stood and posed. There was a large painting behind us on the wall — maybe a mural — of a pasture, surrounded by a lush, green forest with blue skies and fluffy clouds above. After a couple minutes, Gary told us he was finished. Everyone smiled and wished us well.

I became worried. Gary had disappeared. My wife told me to relax. Gary's cousin had arrived to give him a ride home.

The next time we saw Gary, he was very excited to show us how he had touched-up the photo. He had *removed* the chip from my tooth as well as the blood stains on my shirt. Also, he had used other digital tricks with cropping and lighting, which better integrated that painting on the wall — so, it almost looked like the group was standing *outside* on a bridge. Overall, Gary did provide us an *interesting* digital collection of photos that he and his cousin had made of our wedding and reception, as well as our hospital visit.

After I finished my story, I offered to show our neighbors the digital photo collection. "Gary actually took a good photo of me falling."

My wife interrupted, "No, let's just look at the photo above the mantel."

We all got up and walked over to the fireplace. On the top of the mantel — surrounded by plastic, purple wisteria flowers — was the *wedding party photo*, which was taken at the hospital.

After they studied the photo, our guests both shrugged as one of them said, "Well, it does sort of look like you're on a bridge."

Everyone laughed as my wife said, "Yeah, at least I did get my group photo on a *bridge*. Now, why don't you tell us about where you were married?"

LETERS FROM SULTANA
Dr. Angela Brunson

March 20, 1865, Andersonville Prison, Georgia

My darling Elizabeth!

We have been separated by this dreadful war for two impossibly long years, and I pray that you have not given up on me long ago. Have no doubt of my constancy, as I fervently await our wedding day. My love for you has never waned, and thoughts of you have sustained me.

I am terribly sorry for my absence and my silence. My brother William and I were captured in battle and taken prisoner. I don't know if you were ever notified, but we suffered for eighteen months under the Rebels in the camp at Andersonville, Georgia. I so longed to write you, but after seizing our every possession, the guards informed us that postage was our responsibility.

I watched thousands of men die in that wretched hell. Despite my great height, I have wasted away to under 100 pounds, but I was fortunate to avoid the illnesses which ravaged half the camp. I will not disclose the horrors I experienced there in this letter, as I am writing with good news.

I am coming home! I was incredulous when I first heard, but the guards returned our belongings and told us to gather for transport. I was amazed to find the stationery you gave me was well-preserved inside my haversack, so I immediately sat and began to write. Since we are leaving shortly, I will conclude this correspondence. My heart races to think that I will see you soon, my love!

Your own affectionate,
Jacob

April 1, 1865, Camp Fisk, Vicksburg, Mississippi

My very dear Lizzie!

When we were released from Andersonville, I never dreamt of the hardships awaiting us on our 400-mile journey. We marched through forests, fields, and marshes in the freezing rain, most of us barefoot and all of us weak beyond description. Looking behind myself, I thought the grave had given up its dead, as hundreds of men hobbled along with sunken eyes, gaunt faces, and skeletal physiques. Many of our men fell dead along our path, and we could do nothing but leave them behind. I caught fever the day we reached the railway, and suffered delirium for a week in the dirty box car. I was told that our train thrice derailed, twice wrecking a couple cars and maiming their occupants, but I have no recollection of that time.

Thank God, I have recovered from my illness in time to enter the parole camp at Vicksburg, Mississippi. What joy I felt as we marched across the Big Black River bridge and hailed the Stars and Stripes floating in the breeze! Other than you, I have never seen anything more beautiful than that glorious emblem of liberty kissed by the sun. Tears flowed as we sang and danced, thanking the Almighty for His deliverance. I need only await my prisoner exchange before I begin my final journey to your arms. You mustn't worry about me anymore, Liz. Camp Fisk is heaven compared to the hell upon earth that was Andersonville. We are provided with food, shelter, clothing, and supplies. I am certain to regain my health with this fine treatment. Hopefully I can be handsome again when I return. I would likely frighten you in my current condition. At least, William tells me so daily. I sometimes wonder if he will tease you like a little brother once we are wed. He sends you his love, as do I.

I am tired from the long journey, so I will bid you farewell for now, my sweet girl.

Your own,
Jacob

∽

April 25, 1865, Camp Fisk, Vicksburg, Mississippi

My dear, dear Lizzie,

The day has come! The officers just announced our departure, and we march to the river in one hour. I will continue this letter as I have time. I am elated at the thought of seeing you!

4:00 P.M., Vicksburg, Mississippi

We marched for a couple hours before we reached the most magnificent view. The Mississippi River is much larger than I imagined. I could hardly see the other side. The locals say this is an uncommon flood, with the river as wide as fifty miles, owing to the destruction of levees during the war. The current is swift, and the water is icy with runoff from the North. I was surprised to see how it looked like a thick brown sludge, nothing like the clear blue waters of the Ohio River back in Marietta. A piece of driftwood barely goes under and completely disappears. Treetops peek out from the mire far from the shore.

The Vicksburg port seems rather busy. One steamboat departed as we arrived, and two more are docked now. I am standing in line behind at least a thousand paroled prisoners, and we appear to all be boarding the same steamer. With an empty ship in proximity, I cannot surmise the reason, but I intend to find out.

6:00 P.M., Steamship *Sultana*, Vicksburg

I am en route to you, my love! Although the accommodations are not ideal. I underestimated the number of soldiers boarding this ship, but I learned from a mate that over 2,500 persons are onboard. I cannot say for certain, but I hear rumors of an inducement to take all of us together. Perhaps some boats are designed for this many passengers, but the *Sultana* is fitted for only 375, including her crew. With 85 boathands and 70 cabin fares already alit, our commanding officers ordered all the soldiers to embark. Add to that the 60 horses and mules and more than one hundred hogs, and the decks began to buckle. Carpenters added extra stanchions to the decks to hold the excess weight, but they still sag visibly.

I noticed a loud racket as I boarded the ship and found a mechanic working on the boiler. He was hammering back a bulge and patching it with a thin metal plate. I inquired of its effectiveness, and he admitted this was merely a temporary fix. As long as the boilers remain full, it should easily take us to Cairo, Illinois. I worry that the boat is top-heavy with people, as every time we turn, I feel as though we will topple over. I noticed the steamer careening when too many soldiers gathered on one side to greet a passing ship. Over fifty tons of sugar on the cargo deck have kept us upright so far, but we have at times moved with only one wheel, as the other was out of the water.

Many of the prisoners are angry, complaining they have been packed on like hogs or crowded like a flock of sheep. Lizzie, you would be amused by our condition. Every inch of the *Sultana* is jammed full. Men lie on the wheelhouses and guardrails, and they are so thickly packed on the decks that I cannot see the floors. I cannot walk without stepping on a soldier! Even the ship's captain was required to crawl around on the rail to reach his stateroom. The men are indignant to be treated with such unkindness by their own officers, especially when an empty ship was available. I might expect a riot if we were not elated with thoughts of going home, and still physically weak.

Our next stop is Memphis. I am counting the moments until I can hold you in my arms.

April 27, 1865, Steamship Sultana, Memphis, Tennessee

It is after midnight and we have departed Memphis, after unloading the sugar and taking on some coal. The ship is quiet except for choruses of snoring. I cannot sleep. I feel uneasy. I assume my excitement over seeing you is to blame. Last night William and I lay between coils of rope near the flagstaff, but some comrade has occupied that place tonight. Six boys from my regiment offered to make room for us near the boilers, but that was not favorable to my mind. If the ship should explode, anyone on that deck would awake high in the sky. I now sit on the stairway, writing to my sweetheart....

Liz, something happened! A tremendous explosion! Are we being attacked? No, I believe it was the boiler. I smell smoke!

My darling, this may be the end for me. I went to see what happened, and what a sight met my gaze! Three of the boilers exploded violently, sending the nearby soldiers flying into the dark waters. Steam tore through the decks above leaving a gaping hole and turning the decks into shards of shrapnel. The pilot house and Texas collapsed into the ship's furnace. The smokestacks fell, crushing many in the wreckage. The upper decks, crowded with shocked men, were no longer supported. I could only watch as they toppled into the flaming maw that yawned in the center of the ship. As the fire grew, the light revealed a picture that beggars all description. Mangled, scalded bodies in heaps, in all imaginable shapes. Men who piteously begged to be thrown overboard to end their suffering.

If I should survive this night, these sounds shall forever torment me. Oh, that I could shake off this horrible nightmare! You have never heard such screaming. The wailing and moaning, the shrieks and cries, the prayers and groans, the appeals for help are heartrending. I tried to aid a few men who were trapped, but it was impossible to free them. I saw some of the crew jump into the lifeboat, which they overloaded and sank. It seems every man looks out for himself in such disaster.

When the fire broke out, hordes of men rushed to the bow in panic and jumped overboard, tumbling over each other in a churning mass. The river seemed alive with people, clinging to each other and pleading to God as they dragged each other down. I saw 200 men sink at one time and their souls were instantly ushered into eternity. William was determined to jump in, but to enter the water then would have been certain death, so I persuaded him to wait.

Hundreds of us remain on the ship, aware that the river is no kinder than the fire. Our weakened bodies are ill-suited for the frigid water, heavy currents, and too-distant shores. Laboring under such disadvantages, I wonder if anyone can be saved. So, my sweet Elizabeth, I will place this letter securely in my haversack, which I know to successfully protect from water, and I will wait until the water has cleared and the fire is unavoidable. I will find a piece of deck and bravely dive into the ebony muck. I will swim with all my might to reach the unseen shore before the cold overtakes me, thinking always of you. If I do not reach my goal, please forgive my lack of endurance. Know that I love you with all my heart. Do not tarry long in sorrow, and always seek joy in the Lord. I will await our glorious reunion on the streets of gold.

Until we meet again,
Your devoted,
Jacob

I am still alive, my dear, but my situation is precarious. I am perched on a tree branch in the middle of the river. Allow me to explain. When I last wrote, I was huddled on the ship's bow, postponing the inevitable. The fire was slowly overtaking us, but the wind shifted and turned the boat. Suddenly the remaining structure was a raging inferno, and the whole heavens were lighted by the conflagration. The acres of struggling humanity were replaced by 2,000 ghostly, pallid faces drifting lifelessly. The shorelines came into view, and I realized we were nearly a mile from either side.

It seemed my only choices were burning to death or drowning, and there was but little time to be lost. Men were trampling over each other to escape the flames. At first, they threw boards over in an attempt to escape, but then they became frantic and leapt over the rails with no preparation. In panic, they tried to wrestle others from their boards, causing both to go under.

All that remained on the bow were a few bales of hay and the gangplank. William and I joined with about 30 comrades to cut down the bridge and throw it over. I screwed up my courage and prepared to enter what I expected to be my sepulcher. I divested myself of my clothing, took William's hand, and jumped into the icy water 16 feet below. You know I am a strong swimmer, Lizzie, but the currents dragged me deep under the surface. I paddled fervently and reached the top, gasping for air with burning lungs.

I managed only one breath before a drowning man got my neck in a death grip, pulling me back under. I strangled as we sank together into the jaws of death. The frigid water drained my warmth and strength, and my limbs cramped painfully. I had an almost irresistible feeling of drowsiness, and I was on the verge of giving up when I found myself back in Marietta. I heard you call my name and I saw your beautiful face above me. Your hand reached through the inky depths and pulled me to safety.

I rose from my makeshift grave into another nightmare; William was gone. I circled repeatedly, scanning the area for any sign of him, but I could not find him. I screamed for help, but everyone around me was doing the same. My heart was so heavy that I started to sink again. Again, I thought of you and decided I must live.

By the strength of God, I paddled up and swam to the gangplank. Twenty-five men clambered onto the platform, nearly rolling it. I beseeched them to rest on the edges so it would hold all of us without flipping. My words went unheeded, and all but four of them drowned in minutes. The five of us propelled the plank with numb arms and legs. Both shores seemed out of reach, so we moved towards a submerged island with protruding trees. Unless we could escape the water, we would surely perish before help arrived. Each of us clung to a tree and started climbing.

With my exhausted and unfeeling limbs, I struggled to hold on, but managed with great effort to lift myself from the muck. I perched myself securely on the branches and rubbed my arms to bring back the blood flow. Finally out of immediate mortal danger, I took a moment to scan my surroundings. As far as I could see, on every piece of drift, on every tree, bush, or log, I saw a man. The survivors smacked and rubbed themselves to keep warm, but most of the bodies were unmoving. The vastness of this tragedy overwhelmed me, and I was compelled to complete my letter in hopes that relaying my experience to you would console my troubled spirit.

I have alighted on this tree for several hours now. I still hear cries of despair, but they are less frequent. My shivering has calmed considerably, and I am convinced I will survive. I have tried not to look for William's body floating past me, for I don't think I could bear the sight. I see a light in the distance, and I believe it is another steamer. Rescue is nigh!

Your love has saved me, and I am forever grateful!

Jacob

∽

April 30, 1865, Overton Hospital, Memphis, Tennessee

Elizabeth, my sweet angel!

The compassion of the Memphis people is a blessing from above! Every ship in the region rushed to our aid, while civilians on both sides of the river used their private boats or built rafts to reach the survivors. The steamer *Marble City* plucked me from the tree around 9:00 A.M.

Once out of the water, my body alerted me to my many injuries. The pain and weariness overcame me, and I lost consciousness. When I awoke, a kind woman had dressed me in dry clothes and sprinkled flour over my burns to relieve the suffering. She made me drink two horns of whiskey, which warmed me from within. Do not fret, Lizzie! I have fared better than most. My wounds will heal with time.

When we reached Memphis, it appeared that every vehicle in town was at the landing to provide transportation to the hospital. An ambulance conveyed me to Overton Hospital, where I have recovered for three days. I am in a ward with about fifty soldiers, and while I am grateful that my condition is not critical, I lie in anguish for the men around me. Some of them were so severely scalded that they hardly had any skin left. Their agonizing cries were more distressing than you can imagine, but most of them found relief in death within mere hours.

I am told that about 600 survivors were rescued and taken to hospitals. About 200 of those have died from their injuries. I am eager to see if any of my comrades made it, but the doctors say I am too weak to leave. I have been walking around the hospital all morning to show I am ready, but I tell you secretly that I am paying for it. I will lie down for a spell and continue my correspondence later.

I visited several hospitals within blocks of here, each more horrifying than the last. Of the twelve men in my company, only two survived. I checked every bed for a recognizable face. At the fifth hospital, when I was losing hope, I heard a familiar voice call my name. It was William! He is alive! Oh, joyous day! Though we were sinners, the Lord smiled on us. We both have been released to travel home, so I am on my way to you, my dear. Although we have elected to avoid the river and take the train this time.

Soon, my love, soon!
Jacob

WE WILL REMEMBER
Annette G. Teepe

Welcome young sapling! First, let me introduce myself – the folks who work here say I am a 200-year-old White Oak tree. As one of the ancients here, it is my responsibility to pass on my knowledge to the younger generations. Today, I will tell you about life at Elmwood Cemetery and some of the human history in Memphis.

As you can see, the area we live in is beautiful, with rolling hills, flowers, and many trees. When I was about 30 years old, in 1852, Memphis chose this place to establish a fine memorial park. I know 30 years old sounds old to you!

I see the tremble of your leaves. You laugh now, but someday *you* will be much older!

How they named this place is a funny story. People gathered here under my branches and placed their suggestions in a hat, with the agreement that the submission they pulled out would be the name of the cemetery. The paper plucked from the hat said Elmwood Cemetery.

The men who put up the money to buy the land were pleased with the name but had a problem – there were no elms here! They had to have elm trees brought in from somewhere else. Just like you were brought here!

This is a wonderful place to live. Our days are spent soaking up energy from the sun, drinking plentiful water from the ground, and being home to squirrels and birds. We also see plenty of people. Although we can't communicate, we learn to understand them over time. I find people to be a bit fragile, emotional, and erratic but fascinating.

Funerals are important events that happen here. These are often tearful ceremonies to remember the person being laid to rest. Humans miss one another when their time on Earth is done.

We trees know life is a cycle. We come from the earth, live for a time, and return to the ground. We are okay with this. Humans are not always as content with their fate. They like to mark their passing and, today, there are over 75,000 inhabitants here, some who were quite famous in the human world.

Not all the reasons to come here are sad. We are often the backdrop for family photos, wedding pictures, and shade for picnics. People enjoy chatting and exploring history while walking along our trail. These various events mean I have seen people in their best moments as well as their greatest heartbreaks. I have learned a lot about people and will share some of it with you.

For many years I have listened to people sitting together on the benches and sharing memories of those who went before them. Also, I talk to the other trees. Humans recently figured out that we communicate through our roots, using fungi to send messages. We can't send messages to humans, though.

Most times we stand silently by; but there have been times when, if humans had been tuned-in to us, they would have known our sympathy. Our leaves reacted to gentle breezes and gusts of wind to create mournful sounds that could be heard in the background of their own suffering.

We learned the heart and soul of people while observing them during and after the deadliest yellow fever event in Memphis. We were silent witnesses to profound examples of suffering and strength. After experiencing the loss of 2,000 people from yellow fever in 1873, Memphians panicked when the disease came again in 1878.

City trees sent messages telling us that people left their homes, with doors wide open, and took only what they could carry. They fled to cities far away from Memphis. Sadly, word came back through the trees that some people unknowingly took the disease with them, and it spread throughout the Lower Mississippi Valley.

As we watched in silent horror, we discovered this yellow fever epidemic was more deadly than its predecessors. At funerals, we heard that people felt fine on Friday, were violently sick by Saturday, and were dead by Sunday. Terrified cemetery workers buried the bodies as fast as they could, afraid they would catch the disease. Nobody knew why people were dying or what to do to stop the spread.

I can feel through your roots, young sapling, shallow though they may be, that you have great sympathy for the fever's victims.

City officials thought yellow fever spread through the air. To prevent disease, people shot rockets midair to clean it in hopes of stopping the mounting deaths. Day after day, men gathered to set up cannons and prepare rockets. They grimly worked to fire as many as possible into the sky. The sound frightened the birds and squirrels living in my branches. None of us could hide from the shock waves.

Despite the thundering echoes in the sky, the ground continued to fill with those who lost their battle with yellow fever. Loved ones cried beside fresh graves and tried to find hope during the terror. Tears tracked down their faces, wet their handkerchiefs, and dripped into the soil to my roots. I could taste their pain in the tears taken up through my root hairs.

There were amazing acts of kindness during this dreadful time. Compassion shone in the faces of those who stayed in Memphis to help those who were sick. Nuns and doctors worked tirelessly and without care of who they were trying to save. Color, background, or religion didn't matter.

Nurses, doctors, and nuns even came from far away to tend the sick. While many others fled for their lives, these brave souls arrived ready to help fight the disease. Those who visited the graves said they were grateful for the offers of help but felt it might be too little, too late. Nobody knew how to prevent the devastating losses.

By August, the death rate reached seventy in one day, overwhelming the caretakers. There simply weren't enough people to help the sick. There were no painkillers or cures for this disease. Each person either survived or died. All the doctors and nurses could do was provide comfort and take care of them as best they could.

Many who gave their lives trying to care for and save others, are buried here. These people are known as the Martyrs of Memphis. Four of them are Sisters Constance, Thecla, Ruth, and

Frances who share a headstone, with their graves in the shape of a cross.

Since few healthy people were available to properly bury the dead, individual graves were not always an option. There is a place here called "No Man's Land" where around 1,500 unidentified people are buried together in a mass grave. There are no elaborate markers here, mostly an open field.

Our spirits were crushed as we watched people come to visit the graves of their loved ones but not find them. Some had even paid for headstones, but they were not there. These people had nowhere to sit and talk or to leave flowers, so they chose random places to honor their loved ones.

Mississippi River trees told us Memphis had been quarantined. No ships were stopping at our harbor. This was necessary to prevent the spread of disease to other cities but increased the pain in Memphis. Supplies of all types, including food, were running out quickly. No jobs were available for those who could work, and starvation was a real threat.

In late October, as my leaves began to change color, a hard frost hit, and the disease finally ended. Memphis was given relief and a chance to recover. Over 17,000 people had caught the fever and more than 5,000 died. The fever did not kill equally; white people were much more likely to die.

We heard the frustration of Memphians, who felt the loss of their city charter in 1879, due to economic devastation and loss of population. A once vibrant city now had to work together to rebuild.

We watched as Memphis, a city where now seventy percent of the people were black, worked to bring their city back to life. City officials assigned blacks to clean up the streets, bury the dead, clean up the dumps, and spread lime over the vacant lots. There was much to admire as black people completed most of the physical labor to revitalize the city.

A young black man came to visit the grave of his wife and spoke with pride about being one of the first black patrolmen in Memphis. He said he served well, established order, and helped the city heal. He was assigned to patrol in the black neighborhoods and felt good to be helping improve their own neighborhoods. Now everyone knew black patrolmen were capable. He proudly stated, "We will be remembered for that."

In 1912, a great procession came past me, walking under my branches. Five young black men, one carrying a cross, led a procession to a burial site. A large group of people, some weeping, some celebrating his life, followed the casket. This person was certainly important to many people.

As the service began, I learned the person was Robert Reed Church Sr, an influential Memphian. Many people spoke during the funeral to celebrate Robert's life.

One person said, "Robert was a smart businessman and investor. He will always be remembered as being the first black millionaire in the South."

Another man stood up and said, "Thanks to Robert Reed we were able to get loans and build businesses because he founded Solvent Savings Bank, the first black-owned bank."

Others proclaimed him great because he built a park, playground, auditorium and other amenities blacks could enjoy. They said their lives were immeasurably improved by the opportunity to have resources they had previously been denied.

An older man stood up and proudly said, "Robert will be remembered most for saving Memphis. When Memphis lost its city charter after the yellow fever outbreak, our population was decimated, and we were in massive debt. Robert stepped forward and bought the first bond to restore the city charter in 1893."

The crowd clapped and cheered.

"His faith in Memphis inspired others to purchase bonds and help invest in the future of our city. We will be forever grateful to have regained our charter in 1893. Thank you, Robert!"

The people were saddened by Church's passing but celebrated his life and positive influence on Memphis. He is buried in his family's mausoleum, right here next to us. I am honored to shade his final resting place. We will keep his legacy alive by handing this story down from generation to generation.

New stories are told here every day. We remember the past but also learn from, and honor, the present. Let's look around and see what is going on here today.

See the families walking among the monuments and reading the epitaphs? They are here to honor those who passed, whether from their family or not. The young woman placing flowers by the headstone has a soft smile; she is remembering good times with the person she misses.

The older man painting the angel's likeness is memorializing a thing of beauty. The photographer is working to get just the right angle to show the stone structures in their best light. Over there, a naturalist studies us, the trees.

Trees are very important at Elmwood Cemetery, young one. There are 60 species of trees throughout this beautiful place. Many, like you, were donated to honor or memorialize someone who was greatly respected and/or loved. So, stand proudly and grow strong.

Yes, like that. Reach for the sun.

Young sapling, you will hear many people ask, "Will *I* be remembered?" You will see they are remembered. When people come to visit, they sit among the stones beneath our branches, read the epitaphs, and share memories of those who went before them, just as you see today. It is our responsibility to hear their stories. And to remember.

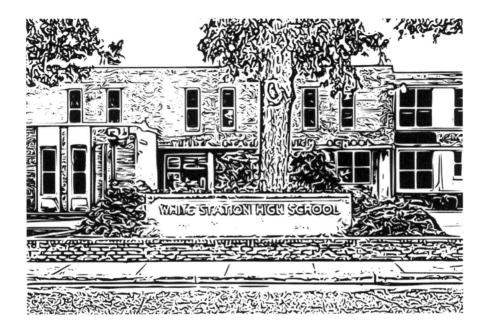

I'LL PAINT THE LILIES
Larry Fitzgerald

Andy Burton and Lily White, two high school seniors attending White Station High School in Memphis, Tennessee, sat on a sofa at Lily's home, staring at a half-finished canvas perched on an easel. Extremely attractive at five feet four inches tall, auburn-haired Lily carefully dipped a tiny brush into a small yellow paint vessel and stared momentarily at the canvas.

"Let's get busy, Andy. Help me find all the eights."

"Will do, but you'll be doing most of them. They are too small for me." Andy was a handsome, red-headed eighteen-year-old. He was five feet ten and still growing.

"Yes, lots of white, red, and yellow flowers." Lily smiled as she pointed to a photograph of a large city fronted by a beautiful park, a peaceful river, and two bridges. "We must get this finished before school ends."

Andrew and Lily, their love blossoming since eighth grade, were on the brink of a new life chapter. Graduation, a mere four weeks away, was a mix of anticipation and bittersweetness. They were bright, excited about life, deeply in love, and extremely happy—except for one major problem. Lily had a full-ride scholarship offer from the University of Tennessee in Knoxville, and Andy had one from the University of Memphis.

Andy and his parents had grappled with the dilemma over the past school year. Their discussions, often held in the kitchen of their modest three-bedroom home in Germantown, a bedroom community of Memphis, were impassioned. Their "absolute final discussion" on the matter was currently underway.

"Mom, Dad. I'll get a job in Knoxville," Andrew insisted. "I don't need a scholarship."

"How will you get a job in Knoxville when you don't have a car to drive?"

"Simple, I'll take Elsie."

"Andrew, please! We have been through this so many times I've lost count. Even if we could afford the tuition, which we can't, you would not have a car in Knoxville. You cannot take the Land Cruiser because your brother will need something to drive here, and without a car to get you back and forth, your job prospects are minimal, at best. And even if you did get a job, you probably wouldn't be able to keep your grades where they need to be to keep your scholarship. I'm sorry, son. It's just not realistic."

Jenny Burton, a petite forty-nine-year-old mother of two teenage boys, wiped her hands on her apron, walked over to Andy, put her arm around his shoulders, and said, "I'm sorry, son. I know you and Lily love each other, and if God means for you to marry, it will happen. And if it's not meant to be...well, you'll have to accept that."

"I can't accept that, Mom! I'll quit school and move to Knoxville first."

"Okay, Andrew," Jenny fumed with an air of finality. "Suit yourself. But I want you to know I have had it with this subject. No more discussion!"

Andrew's dad, Phil, sat on a bar stool at a counter that divided the den from the kitchen. This discussion was nothing new to him, but it had reached the point where he felt compelled to speak.

"Andy, let's take a practical look at this. You have a full-ride academic scholarship for a degree in computer science at the University of Memphis. You have free room and board here; with the scholarship, that's fifty thousand dollars saved annually. That's money in the bank, son. When you and Lily get married, you will have no debt. And if you both get jobs while in school, you will have a strong financial foundation from the get-go. Doesn't that make perfect sense?"

Andy sat down and considered his dad's point. Then he softly uttered, "That makes sense, Dad. But here's my problem. If Lily goes off to UT without me, she will have every guy on campus asking her out, and I'm afraid I'll lose her. The thought of that makes me sick to my stomach. I don't think I could handle it. That's my problem, Dad."

Phil paused for several seconds, rubbed his chin, and reasoned, "Well, son, then we're back to those words your mom mentioned: 'If it's meant to be.' Listen, Andy, your mom and I are proud of how you and Lily have maintained your relationship. Over the years, your dates have mostly been doing your painting at our home or hers. You didn't go out and spend lots of money. You had fun just being together. We see that as a sign of a lasting relationship. You don't have to worry about losing Lily. A separation might even be good for your relationship."

Andy stood, pushed his chair into the table, and said, "Thanks, Dad." Then he walked over to his mom, now in the kitchen. He put his arm around her and whispered. "I love you, Mom."

Teary-eyed, Jenny Burton returned the hug and sighed, "I love you, son."

⊷

Over the summer months, Andy and Lily continued painting. They cherished their time together. They would shoot baskets, walk or ride bicycles through neighborhood parks, and occasionally watch a local movie. But most of their time was spent painting.

As departure drew near, everyone gathered at the Burtons for an outdoor barbeque, the young couple's favorite food. After a delicious meal, Phil Burton and Stanley White went into the den to watch the Chicago Cubs play the St. Louis Cardinals. Andy, Lily, and younger brother Tim Burton went outside to shoot hoops. Joy White and Jenny Burton disappeared into the kitchen for the after-dinner clean-up.

While carefully wiping dry an ice cream bowl, Joy said, "It's been a fun day, Jen. But my gosh, where has the summer gone? These kids will be in college next week."

"I know. It's hard to believe, isn't it?"

Joy put the bowl in the open cupboard and chose another one. "What do you think will happen to our kids, Jen? Are they going to make it?"

"I hate to be negative, but young romance doesn't usually survive, especially when there's separation."

Joy placed the bowl in the cupboard and mused, "They seem so committed to each other...now, anyway."

"Yes, but there will be a different atmosphere in college, especially for Lily. We'll see. Anyway, you and I will be around to pick up the pieces if there are any."

Jenny dried her hands on a kitchen towel and turned to Joy. "They are two very innocent and naïve kids. Let's be sure we stay in touch with each other, Joy, for their sake."

Hugging Jenny tightly, Joy whispered, "For sure."

Andy drove Lily home that evening. He felt deep emotions as he entered the White's driveway. He was happy to be in a nice car, sitting next to the girl he loved. But his heart was breaking, knowing he would not see Lily again for almost four months.

Andy parked the car, set the emergency brake, pulled Lily into his arms, and kissed her passionately. "I love you, Lily."

"I love you too, Andy. I will miss you very much. Do you promise to text me every day?"

"Yes. If you answer every time."

"I will. I promise."

"Even if you're in class?"

"No. I'll have to wait until class is over."

"How about if you're at a frat party?"

"Maybe. If I'm not jiving with some cool fraternity dude."

"That's not funny."

"Sorry."

"No fraternity dudes! I don't want to have to come and get you. That would be embarrassing."

"No worries. None of those fraternity dudes will be interested in me."

"Don't kid yourself. Just remember your painting pal, who's waiting for you to come back home. Okay?"

"And what about you? What will you be doing in your spare time?"

"Studying."

"Good."

The teens continued snuggling together until the patio lights flashed on and off, signaling Lily to come in and Andy to go home.

Over the next three and a half months, hundreds of texts, emails, and phone calls filled the airwaves between Knoxville and Memphis. Assurances of love and commitment and complaints of homework, boredom, and separation were topics shared daily. But, in early December, communications shut down. On the night of December 11, Andy, having not heard from Lily for several days, sat on his bed and dialed her number. No answer.

I don't understand, but she'll be home next week. I can't wait. She can explain it all then.

On December 18, Joy White answered her phone. "Hello. This is Joy."

"Hi, Mrs. White. This is Andy."

"Hello, Andy. How are you?"

"Good, thank you. What time will Lily be home?"

"Well, her dad is picking her up today. I'm not sure when they will leave, but they'll arrive late. Why don't you call back tomorrow afternoon when she has gotten some sleep and had a chance to settle in."

Tomorrow afternoon? Are you kidding me? I'm dying here, lady. Come on!

Andy spent the rest of Wednesday shopping for a gift for Lily. He knew finding the perfect gift would be difficult because he detested shopping. He considered a nice canvas and frame for a future picture they could paint together but decided against it.

No, this has to be special.

After several hours of shopping, Andy bought Lily a three-hundred-dollar necklace on credit. He spent the rest of the day washing and vacuuming Elsie, preparing for his date with Lily that afternoon.

"Thanks for washing my ride, my brother," Tim sang out as he came off the front porch of the Burton home down to the driveway where Andy was wiping down the old Land Cruiser.

Andy straightened up and faced his sibling. "In your dreams, bro. This is my car today and tonight. Don't even touch it until I'm through using it."

"We'll see. I might have to speak to a higher authority."

"You just did, Timmy."

"Eww. Kind of salty there, bro. What bougie place are you taking her to tonight?"

"Don't know. Maybe Henri's."

"Aww. Big bucks."

∽

Andy was nervous as he dialed Lily's number. It had been so long since they had spoken, and he was desperate to hear her voice. He wanted her assurance that all was well between them, but his phone call went unanswered.

"That does it!" Andy jumped into Elsie and headed to Lily's.

On arrival, he walked to the front door and rang the doorbell. Minutes later, Lily slowly opened the door. She wore a sweatsuit with an orange UT emblazoned across the front. Lily was pale and appeared to have been crying.

"Hello, Andy. Uh, would you like to come in?"

Andy stepped inside as Lily closed the door behind him.

Lily led the way into the family room and turned toward Andy. He stepped up to Lily and embraced her. "I've missed you, babe," Andy whispered. "Are you okay?"

"Yes. I'm just…tired. Please, sit down." Lily pointed to a leather recliner. Andy felt repelled. He continued to stand while Lily settled into a side chair.

"What's going on, Lily? Why are you ghosting me all of a sudden? Is there another guy?"

There was a long pause. When Lily finally responded, she said, "I'm sorry, Andy. I'm just going through some difficult things right now. I need time to think them through."

"What's that supposed to mean? Am I persona non-grata now?"

Lily's eyes watered up. "No, we can talk, Andy. It's just that I need…Well, I need some time to myself right now. I'm sorry, Andy. I truly am."

"I don't get it, Lily. You promised you would stay true to me. Did you lie to me? What's going on? Is there another guy? Tell me, Lily! Is there another guy? What's his name?"

Lily didn't respond. Tears gushed from her eyes.

After several minutes, Andy spoke quietly, "So, you have nothing to say, Lily? After what we have been through together. All the promises. All the time. You have nothing to say? Who are you now, anyway?"

With tears streaming from her eyes, Lily bellowed, "I don't know who I am, Andy."

"What do you mean you don't know who you are? What's happened to you, Lily?"

Lily, confused and weeping uncontrollably, gazed at Andy and whimpered, "I'm pregnant, Andy."

Andy was stunned. His heart sank into his gut. He wobbled. "YOU'RE WHAT???

Lily doubled over, sobbing hysterically. "I can explain," she blurted out incoherently. "I was at a party and oh, my dear Andy, I am so sorry."

Andy was shellshocked. His only response was, "You're pregnant?"

With tears streaking down her face, Lily looked up and nodded. "I can explain, Andy. Please... I was... I was..."

Andy paused momentarily and staggered to the door. "I need to go," which he did, leaving Lily in despair.

※

Over the ensuing months, Lily dropped out of college and, on February 14, delivered her baby, a healthy girl she named Valerie Joy. For the following year, Lily lived at home but then moved into an apartment and, with her parents' help, opened a small painting studio where she sold paintings and taught painting crafts to local budding artists.

Andy also dropped out of college and disappeared completely. A year later, he resurfaced in Germantown wearing a Navy Seals uniform. He spent thirty reclusive days at home before being shipped overseas to join a command post in the Middle East.

FIVE YEARS LATER

Twenty-two-year-old Tim Burton bounced down the stairway and into the family kitchen.

"Good morning, son," Jenny Burton said as Tim tiptoed forward and gave her a peck on the cheek. "Will you have time for breakfast before you go to the airport?"

"Don't think so. Andy's plane's due in an hour, and I can't be late picking him up."

"I wish we were all meeting him."

"I know, Mom. But that's not what Andy wanted."

"He's going to need a lot of help getting his stuff together, son."

"I know. I got this, Mom."

※

Tim Burton carefully hugged his brother when they met at Memphis International Airport. Andy was in full dress uniform, with a chest full of medals. But Andy's left sleeve was empty. He wore a prosthesis for his left leg, and his face was severely scarred.

"It's good you're home, Andy. The folks are anxious to see you."

❧

That evening, Andy pulled into a handicapped parking space in front of an art studio. He observed people inside, hovering over canvasses. Andy exited the car and, with great effort, made it to the entrance. Steadying himself with his cane, he opened the door and stepped inside. Lily White appeared immediately, and the two former sweethearts stood face to face for the first time in six years.

Both were overwhelmed with indescribable emotions. Lily knew Andy had been severely wounded. *"But not this badly, dear Lord. Maybe he was wrong, but he didn't deserve this." What can I say to him? How can I help him? Should I even try?*

Andy had dreamed of this day over many months of hospital care and the grueling rehab he had endured. *I am so sorry. I let her down in her darkest hour. I was so wrong. Will she ever forgive me?*

"May I help you," Lily stammered.

"I'd like to inquire about taking lessons."

Lily waivered. Then she said, "Uhm, maybe I can find a place for you." She walked to a far corner of the studio and pointed to an open table. As Andy sat down, Lily murmured, "What are you doing here?"

"Like I said, I want to learn how to paint."

"Why are you doing this, Andy Burton?"

"My specialty is flowers. Especially lilies."

"Yeah, right. There's the canvas. Start painting." Lily turned away.

"Will you come back and check on me?"

"We close at 9."

By 8:30 p.m., every student was gone except for Andy. He was busy stroking his canvas when Lily walked back to his table. She leaned against a post and asked again, "Why are you here?"

Andy put his brush down, leaned back, and began to speak. "Well, the truth is, Lily, I came here to tell you how sorry I am for running out on you when you needed me most."

Lily didn't respond, but her eyes suddenly became damp.

"I saw you then as damaged goods. I could not imagine any way forward for us. For me, it was over. I realize that was selfish and stupid, but at the time, I wanted my life to end. I would have ended it myself, but I didn't have the courage. I signed up to become a Navy Seal and volunteered for every dangerous mission that came up, hoping to be killed in combat. But God spared me, and, at the same time, he taught me a critical life lesson."

Andy paused for a moment, then said, "Such irony. Look at me, Lily! What do you see? Am I not the very embodiment of damaged goods?"

Lily looked at Andy through teary eyes. Then she disappeared for several minutes, returning with two paintings. One was of Andy in full dress uniform, complete with his medals.

"What's this?" he asked.

"Your mom gave the picture to my mom."

"So, you painted it."

"Yes, Andy. I was so proud of you despite what happened between us."

Andy gulped. "Thank you."

"Here's another painting." Lily held up a canvas of Valerie Joy, her six-year-old daughter. "This is my precious little girl. She is a gift from God."

"Beautiful. I want to meet her."

"Maybe you will, but now I must close the store and pick her up from Mom and Dad's."

"I haven't finished painting my lilies. May I come back tomorrow?"

"We're closed tomorrow."

"Oh."

"Lily put the pictures aside and said, "Would you repeat the question you asked?"

"What question?"

"The one about what I see when I look at you?"

Andy slowly rose to his feet. "When you look at me, Lily, what do you see?"

Lily's eyes locked into Andy's. She said softly, "I see the man I have loved ever since I was in the eighth grade."

Andy stepped forward and pulled Lily into his arms.

PROMENADE AT THE PEABODY
Ruth Ashcraft Munday

"Left, right, left, right. You've got it, Jill. I think you have been practicing your marching skills. Now, let's roll out the red carpet," Mollie said.

Chattering with excitement, Mollie and Jill worked together to unfurl the regal red rug.

"Well done, young ladies, time to head to the elevator," said the man in the red and gold jacket.

Smoothing their dresses, the sisters stood up and turned to face The Peabody Hotel Duckmaster.

"We're ready," they said.

He handed them each a white cane topped with a bronze duck head and set the red-carpeted stairs in place by the fountain. A crowd was starting to gather in the hotel lobby. Murmurs of various conversations rippled through the air as guests claimed their seats. Eager children bordered the crimson path extending from the lobby elevator to the majestic travertine marble fountain. The hands of the Grandfather Clock moved closer to the appointed time. It was almost 11o'clock!

"Ladies and Gentlemen, please welcome our Honorary Duckmasters, Mollie and Jill. We will return shortly with the 'World-famous Peabody Ducks' for their traditional morning march," the Duckmaster said.

Jill's eyes twinkled with anticipation. She ran ahead of the others to the elevator and hurriedly punched the up arrow several times in a row. As the lobby elevator doors opened, Jill raced in and pressed the rooftop button. Mollie and the Duckmaster leapt in before the doors snapped closed. Numbered floor lights blinked as they rose up, up, up to their destination.

"Jill, how did you know where to go? Why are you trying to get there ahead of us?" Mollie said.

Jill's heart went racing as she wondered if she should tell Mollie and the Duckmaster about her new friend. Jill thought back to last night. Was it a dream? Or, did it really happen? The adventure began to replay in her mind...

Clad in a ruffly blue nightgown, Jill twirled on the dance floor of The Skyway Room. Lost in thoughts of her favorite fairy tale princess, she did not notice the long panels of silvery-colored curtains swaying and rustling in the far corner. A feathery shadow rhythmically fluttered on the wall.

"Quack, may I have this dance?" a raspy voice said, and out popped a duck with a shiny green head.

Mid-twirl, Jill eyed the creature warily as it moved from behind the curtain to the top of a nearby chair.

"Hi there, I'm Michael Mallard. I have a few dance moves of my own I can show you. Ever heard of the 'webbed foot wiggle' or the 'yellow bill boogie'? I'm known as the ultimate 'disco duck.' How about I 'take you under my wing' and spin you around? Wak-wak-wak, I quack myself up," he said.

Jill grinned and ran over to her new dance partner. Round and round and round the chair she went, 'ducking' under his wing and cavorting about, imitating his unique style, until she collapsed on the floor in giggles. Michael flew down and landed beside her.

"What's a little girl like you doing out on her own at such a late hour?"

"I slipped out of bed and visited different floors of the hotel. The elevator zoomed fast at night with no one else around. I peeked in all the ballrooms looking for the perfect place to twirl. The Skyway Room is my favorite. I like being up high, closer to the stars. I wish I could fly like you. How come you can talk?"

"Go look out the open window."

Jill jumped up and skipped over to look outside. She leaned out the window and craned her neck to observe the luminous night sky.

"Wow! The moon is as big as a princess pumpkin carriage.

Does it give you magical powers?"

"Yes, it's a blue supermoon. See how the moonbeams are shooting down to Earth. If an animal swallows a blue 'supermoonbeam', the gift of speaking is granted from midnight until dawn. I happened to be the lucky duck that had a 'light meal,' wak-wak-wak, get it, and digested photons of golden goodness."

"You're funny. Do you think if the blue supermoon can make you talk, it could make me a princess?"

"I don't know about that, but I dub you Princess of The Royal Duck Palace. It's just beyond the The Skyway Room on the Roof Top. Shall we go stroll through the kingdom?"

"Yes, I would like that. But, I'm not a duck. May I be Princess of the Peabody?"

"Grand idea! Princess of the Peabody, it is. Shall we promenade through the Peabody? I will be going back to the farm soon, and I wish to explore more of the hotel. You just happened to catch me at the beginning of my moonlight adventure. Want to join me?"

"Oh yes, I'd love to walk with you and pretend it's my castle. But, wait a minute, I thought you lived here at the Peabody?"

"I'm a Roof Top resident for now, along with my four sisters. We're all Mallards. We live at The Royal Duck Palace for three months, and then swap out with a new group of five ducks, fresh from our family farm."

"I like hearing about your family, please tell me more."

"Well, the tradition of the Peabody Ducks goes all the way back to the 1930s. As a joke, a hotel manager placed three live ducks in the Peabody lobby fountain. Instead of chaos, it became beloved entertainment for the guests. The original ducks were named Gayoso, Chisca, and Peabody, to commemorate the three hotels owned by the Memphis Hotel Company. Those three ducks were eventually replaced with five Mallards. Peabody Duck names are no longer shared in public. Now, we just go by the names our parents give us at the farm."

"Oh, okay. My parents named me Jill, and my sister, Mollie. Mollie told me that in the morning, the ducks will march to some music. Quack, quack, quack."

Jill strutted around and flapped her arms.

"She's right. In 1940, a former circus animal trainer worked as a bellman at the hotel, and he volunteered to care for my ancestors and taught them how to walk the red carpet. He served as the first official Duckmaster for over 50 years and even added the special music of John Phillip Sousa's 'King Cotton March'."

"You're one smart duck!"

"Thank you. I do have my 'Ducktorate' in Peabody History, wak-wak-wak."

"I wish I could bring you to school for show-and-tell."

"Well, I'll show you how to march and you can tell your friends at school."

"Da da da da da da...follow me Jill, left, right, left right, you're a natural! Let's march over to The Royal Duck Palace and I will introduce you to my sisters, Maren, Millie, Malon, and Merri Mallard. Over 1,500 Mallard ducks in my family have had the honor of entertaining guests at the Peabody over the years. Some of my relatives have even been featured on television shows and magazine covers."

"Wow, that's a dynasty of ducks! What happens when you go back to the farm?"

"We return to our 'wild ways' and just enjoy doing ducky things. Swimming in the pond, scratching around the yard, eating grains, and of course, telling stories of our time at the Peabody."

"Who do you tell your stories to?"

"The other ducks, of course. We can understand each other. Many well-known dignitaries and celebrities have passed through the doors of The Peabody Hotel. My Great Uncle Merlin told the best story. He had a magical blue supermoon night with Elvis Presley. Elvis had just signed with RCA Records while here at the Peabody. Great Uncle Merlin was one of the ducks that marched through the lobby that day. Elvis was up on the Mezzanine watching the parade and caught his eye. He later saw Elvis strolling out on the Roof Top. It was after midnight. Great Uncle Merlin had just swallowed a blue 'supermoonbeam' and went flying around the corner of The Royal Duck Palace, when he crashed into

Elvis. He landed in a rumpled heap of feathers on top of Elvis' blue suede shoes. Great Uncle Merlin jokingly said, 'At least it was a soft landing'. Wak-wak-wak. When he recounted Elvis' amusement over a talking duck, he recalled that Elvis said, 'better stay off of my blue suede shoes!' After they chatted, Elvis said, 'Hey, I've gotta song I want to run by you that I plan to release next year.' He began singing a silly version of 'Blue Suede Shoes' that used the words, 'go duck go,' instead of 'go cat go.' After sharing laughs, they roamed downtown Memphis and talked until dawn. Elvis walked him back to The Royal Duck Palace, with a serenade of 'Blue Moon'. It was a night to remember!"

"I wish I could meet Elvis. I like to dance to his songs."

"Well, Princess Jill, I can't take you to Elvis, but I can take you to a palace. Off we go and out the door. Left, right, left, right."

The sky seemed to sag with the size of the moon and it appeared to be even closer to the horizon. The Royal Duck Palace gleamed in the moonlight.

"The moon is so low I think I could almost touch it. Are your sisters awake?" Jill said.

"Looks like they're sleeping. They do like their beauty rest. I will have to tell them about you later. You can get a look inside our palace, if you stand here. We have an amazing place."

Jill pressed her face to the glass.

"That's a neat bronze duck statue with water coming out of its mouth. Is it named after anyone? You could call it Princess Jill."

"Wak-wak-wak. Maybe you want to be Princess of The Royal Duck Palace after all. Think you could fit inside this miniature version of the Peabody? It even has grass on the front lawn. I like to nap there."

"I'm too tall to be the Princess of that Peabody. I'm ready to go back inside. I'm getting hungry."

"Okay, I know one restaurant we can go to where I'll be safe, Chez Philippe. I've heard they're the only local French restaurant that doesn't list duck on the menu. Whew! I bet we can find a salad in their kitchen. Romaine lettuce is my favorite snack."

"You can have salad; I want a cookie."

"Okay, let's go. To the elevator!"

Jill broke into a run across the Roof Top, through The Skyway Room, and into the waiting elevator. Michael had to fly to catch up with her.

"My wings are faster than my legs. Wak-wak-wak."

They exited the elevator and entered the green carpeted dining area of Chez Philippe.

"Oh, I like their décor. This is fancier than anything I've seen on the farm. I see the kitchen door. Race you to the refrigerator."

Michael flew past Jill through the swinging doors. Jill followed him and opened the refrigerator. Her eyes widened as she took inventory. Cookies, chocolates, and dainty pastries lined the shelves. The drawers were full of fresh salad ingredients. Jill selected a piece of dark green romaine for Michael.

"Delicious lettuce! What dessert will you choose, Princess Jill?"

"Hmm, I pick the cookie with golden icing. It reminds me of the moon. Yum!"

"Speaking of the moon, we'd better keep moving. It will be dawn before we know it. Where do you want to go next?"

"I want to go see the pianos. I'm taking piano lessons and my teacher told me the Peabody has a piano that plays itself and another one that belonged to the man who wrote the 'Star Spangled Banner'."

"I have heard people talk about those pianos when I am swimming around the lobby fountain. The Mezzanine, or 'the Mez' as we ducks like to call it, has one of the pianos you referred to and a memorabilia room. It is full of history just like me, wak-wak-wak."

"What was that 'P' word you used earlier? Prom something?" Jill said.

"Oh yes, promenade—it means a leisurely walk or stroll."

"It sounds like a princess word. Let us promenade through the Peabody to see the pianos."

Michael extended his wing.

"Allow me to escort you to the pianos, Princess Jill. We can promenade together."

Hand-in-wing, they meandered to the Mezzanine, taking in all the grandeur surrounding them as they made their way up the stairs.

"Look, there's a Grand Piano. My teacher would be impressed. The sign says it was originally custom-built for Francis Scott Key, in 1838. That's older than the duck march. I wish I could touch the keys. I know how to play 'Twinkle, Twinkle Little Star'."

"I'm sure you play beautifully. We'd better keep our promenade going. It's getting late. Let's go to the room with all the pictures and artifacts."

"There's a photo of Elvis and his record company," Jill said.

"Yep, just like Great Uncle Merlin said. Many memories adorn these walls. Tonight's adventure will be a special story for me to share back at the farm."

"We have one more piano to find. I heard it making music as we came up the steps."

"You're right. I think it's on the other side of the lobby. Shall we promenade down the stairs?"

"Yes. I hear the Grandfather Clock chiming one-two-three-four. Four in the morning! I've never been up this late."

"It means I only have one more hour. We'd better go find that player piano and then get you back to bed."

Gliding down the stairs, they followed the sound of faint piano music.

"I see it! The keys are playing themselves! Do your dance, Michael."

Michael flew up on top of the piano and broke into the "webbed foot wiggle". Jill sat down on the floor to watch him, and before she knew it, her eyes grew heavy with sleep...Jill next realized she was back in the elevator with Mollie and the Duckmaster. She couldn't remember the end of her adventure.

"The elevator is about to open, Jill. You never did answer my question. Why were you trying to get to the ducks before us?" Mollie said.

"Oh, I just wanted a chance to say hello," Jill said.

The Duckmaster laughed as they stepped off the elevator and

made their way to The Royal Duck Palace.

"You may certainly say hello. However, don't expect anything but a quack back. They don't speak our language. You can use your white canes with the bronze duck heads, to help guide the ducks to the elevator and down the red carpet to the lobby fountain. Once they get in the fountain, we'll feed them their lunch of scratch grains served on a silver platter," the Duckmaster said.

"How many times a day do they eat?" Jill asked.

"Twice a day, off the silver platter. I also give them snacks. Do you know what their favorite snack is?" the Duckmaster said.

"Corn," Mollie said.

"Romaine lettuce," Jill said.

"That's exactly right, Jill. You must have insider information," said the Duckmaster.

He stepped forward and opened the door to The Royal Duck Palace. Jill felt a smile spread across her face.

"Alright duckies, are you ready?" the Duckmaster said.

The ducks came filing out. The four girl ducks fluttered their wings as if to say hi. The duck with the green head was the last to exit. He brushed up against Jill's leg and touched her hand with his wing.

"Jill, I think that duck with the green head likes you," Mollie said.

"I like him too," Jill said, as they made their way back to the elevator.

"I'll push the buttons this time," Mollie said.

Down, down, down they went to the lobby, which was crowded with spectators. As the elevator doors opened and the music began to play, the duck with the green head turned and winked at Jill, as she followed him for a final promenade down the red carpet.

BEST SEAT IN THE HOUSE
Gary Fearon

It felt like I had won the lottery when I opened the nondescript white envelope and retrieved what I had waited three weeks to receive: my MovieFan card. After hearing all the press about customers getting to see unlimited movies in any nationwide theater for 19.99 a month, I could hardly wait to find out if the hype was real or if it was a brilliantly seductive scam.

Admiring the shiny silver card from every angle as if it were a priceless gem, I could only think of my parents and how they would have loved this. Like me, they were avid movie buffs who took me to the Summer Drive-In whenever something good came out. I saw so many films as a kid that I couldn't tell you half of them; they are all one collective memory that makes going to the movies today my version of comfort food. These days, the Malco theater chain continues to feed my appetite via luxurious cinemas featuring leather recliners.

But it wasn't just the siren song of limitless silver screen indulgence now luring me in. After years of just thinking about it during my day job at the shoe store, I decided now was the time to really pursue my dream of becoming a screenwriter. And MovieFan would be my ticket to enable endless research toward that end. I could study story structure, character development, and current trends every night of the week if I chose, all for not much more than the price of a regular movie ticket.

My already-racing heart kicked up a notch when I realized I could try the card out that very night. I downloaded the app to my phone, checked the showtimes, and picked a suspense film. Not my typical first choice, mind you, but what better way to ramp up the thrill of my new filmgoing freedom than with a fright flick?

As promised, my MovieFan card paid for my ticket at the Towne Cinema without incident. Choosing my seat at the self-serve kiosk, I was pleased to see that hardly anyone else had bought tickets to this 7:00 showing, which allowed me to reserve my favorite seat in the house, near the center of the theater. D-7.

Since this was a special occasion, I didn't balk at paying $13 for a popcorn and Coke combo. And as the lights dimmed for the coming attractions, with my mouth full of buttery fluffiness and my feet up on the recliner of my perfectly situated D-7, I thought, *This is the life. My ultimate man cave. I have arrived.*

The scary movie turned out to be just okay, and I learned more from what I felt were its missteps than anything else. Even I could see that the hatchet-wielding heavy had no clear motivation for being a cut-up. But I did enjoy stepping out of my comfort zone and trying something different, which my movie club membership would allow me to do as often as I wanted.

In fact, it got me thinking. Having no idea what my own screenplay was going to be about, this was my chance to experience every genre until I found the one that felt right for me.

I decided to start keeping notes that very night, chronicling what I liked and what I didn't like about each film. Then I tried writing a horror movie scene, showing the early life of a stalker and hinting as to why he ended up the way he did, but I just couldn't get into it. I felt uncomfortable exploring the origins of evil and realized that slasher movies are not in my blood.

At work the next day, all I could think about was this new path I was on: mild-mannered sneaker salesman by day, surreptitious screenwriting student by night. After ringing up my last pair of Nikes at the close of my shift, I was able to make a 7:10 showing of a buddy comedy, which nicely balanced the disquieting scenes from the night before. As luck would have it, I was the only one in the theater. I felt like Steven Spielberg getting a private showing. Even without popcorn, I enjoyed the lap of luxury via the comfort of D-7.

Back home that night, after making my notes in a mostly positive review, I decided to try my hand at writing the opening scene of a buddy comedy. Using some of the formula I had just observed, I came up with an odd couple-style pairing of a straight-laced attorney and the hapless paralegal he gets saddled with. This was a premise overflowing with comedic possibilities, I felt, until I spent four hours on it and realized I know nothing about the legal profession. I needed to get to bed anyway, and there would be plenty more genres to explore.

Spoiled by my previous near-empty viewings, I hadn't expected the theater to be crowded -- much less for my coveted D-7 to be taken -- when the latest action movie came out. I chose the nearest available seat, B-3. It was uncomfortably close to the front and off to the side, but I quickly got used to it, and my proximity to the screen served to intensify the action scenes.

That night I didn't feel particularly creative. My review confirmed that a movie filled with car chases wasn't my speed. But it's possible that much of my disinterest came from craning my neck for two hours and wishing I had attended a different showing.

I'll admit that I was probably way too picky about my seating. But just as a wine connoisseur has pre-sip rituals and holidays have traditions, I had my cinematic sweet spot, and it was D-7.

Which is why I started swinging by the theater during my lunch breaks to reserve D-7 if I had any reason to suspect a crowded showing that night. This tactic worked flawlessly for several weeks. During that time I made a lot of notes and tried writing a lot of scenes covering many different genres. Even so, I still had no good storyline, nor had I identified my ideal genre.

Eventually, the summer blockbusters arrived and I was excited about seeing the new superhero spectacle everyone was talking about. Knowing the theater would be packed on a Friday night, I made my noontime purchase for the 7:00 showing, pleasantly surprised that my seat hadn't already been reserved, as it sometimes was. That night I splurged on popcorn and Coke. Although I was a little late getting there and would be walking in just as the previews were ending, I knew D-7 was waiting for me.

But it wasn't. Row D was completely filled with people, as was every other row in the stadium theater, except for one aisle seat way up in the very back. Between my lateness, the darkness, and my hands being full, I wasn't about to miss anything and grabbed that only available spot. I enjoyed the movie but couldn't stop fuming about the fact that someone had the gall to take my reserved seat. When the movie was over I was going to see who it was and confront them. Depending, of course, on how big they were.

When the closing credits began, row D exited in short order, but I noticed that the occupant of my seat didn't get up right away. Only when the theater had emptied did I see the long hair of a girl wobbling awkwardly in the seat. She leaned from side to side several times as I walked down to her aisle, and her clumsy movements suggested she was drunk. While I'd had over two hours to compose a brief but meaningful reprimand to some inconsiderate guy, I hadn't prepared for an inebriated lady.

When I reached row D, she was still fumbling, and I realized she was trying to reach crutches on the floor.

"Can I help you with that?" I asked, startling her.

"Could you please?" she asked. "I can't get to them."

Her bandaged leg from foot to knee told some of the story. As I handed her the crutches she thanked me, and – with great effort – positioned them under her arms while she rose.

"I'm still not used to these," she said. "I've only had them for two weeks."

116

"It takes time," I encouraged. "I had them once myself."

"I hope I didn't take someone's seat," she said, looking at the back of the theater. "My ticket was for up there, but I just couldn't go any higher with these things."

I almost revealed the situation but chose not to make her feel guilty. "You like the nosebleed section, do you?"

"No," she said, "that was just the only seat left when I bought my ticket. Even the handicapped seats were taken. *This* was a really good seat, though! I may have to get this one from now on."

I changed the subject. "So, how'd you break your leg?"

When she hesitated, I realized I had probably misspoken.

"I was in an accident." Her tone had changed and that seemed to be all she wanted to say about it, so I said something sympathetic and let it go. By now we were at the cinema door, which I held for her as we emerged into the hallway.

"I've got it from here," she said. "Thanks for your help."

"Oh. Okay, well, it was nice meeting you."

I headed to the lobby to get refills on my popcorn and Coke to take home. Suddenly, I wondered about the girl's means of transportation until I saw her at the front exit, getting picked up by someone in a minivan, whose silhouette told me nothing.

That night I didn't make notes. Instead, I finally started my screenplay, a romance about a fellow who meets a mystery girl with crutches who has a story to tell. I haven't gotten far and don't know how it will end, but each time I go to the movies now I reserve D-8, hoping for the next scene.

ERNEST T. BOTTOMWHITE
Nancy Roe

I'm sitting on an orange bucket staring at the most beautiful green eyes I've ever seen on a four-year-old child. Her mother, a tall woman with long blonde strands, stands next to her, taking pictures of the mansion for a photo layout. I overheard the woman talking to the man who is currently renovating Annesdale. The estate got its name, Annesdale, from Colonel Robert C. Brinkley, originator of the Peabody Hotel, when he bought the estate as a wedding gift for his daughter Annie and her husband Colonel Robert Bogardus Snowden. The year was 1868 or 1869. I'm not so good at remembering the years associated with major events. The years have lost meaning to me. Nevertheless, I remember that they dedicated the estate to the daughter by naming it "Annesdale."

The 9,000 square foot home includes a bell tower, grand parlor, sunroom, dining room, kitchen, library, and several bedrooms with eleven fireplaces and a spiral staircase. (Yes, it's big!) Walnut paneling, a marble entryway, hand-painted ceilings, crystal chandeliers, Aubusson window treatments (A stuffy word for exceptional quality flowing fabric with earthy and soft pastel colors. The renovator uses this word quite often.), and fourteen-foot ceilings complete the exquisite mansion. I know every inch of this place. I've had over a century to discover every nook and cranny.

The petite girl with shoulder length curly blonde hair is not like most children I've encountered in the last one hundred and fifty years. She is standing still, tilting her head from side to side, her white dress with red polka dots swaying. I wonder if she has a disability. There is nothing behind me but a solid walnut wall. We play the staring game for a few more minutes before I get bored and walk into the hallway.

Then the most unusual thing happens. The girl follows and

stands next to me. I step into the sunroom and sit on one of six folding chairs the workers have set up for their breaks. The painters added a second coat of white on the walls last night and the fumes faintly linger. Again, she follows and sits on the chair next to the one I have occupied.

"Can you see me?" I say. Then I laugh because it would be absurd. To my utter surprise, she laughs too, then says, "Why do you wear funny clothes?"

I choke, having held my breath for too long. How is it possible this girl can see me? "This is my uniform from the Civil War," I say. "This is what I was wearing when I died." Perhaps I shouldn't have said such a morbid thing to a small child.

But the little girl shows no signs of being fazed. "If you're dead, why aren't you in heaven?" she asks. "My doggy went to heaven last week."

"That is an excellent question," I say, then smile. I have no answer for her.

She smiles in return. "My name is Penny. What's your name?"

I sit up straight, realizing I haven't had to flex my manners in so long, I've forgotten how to be a gentleman. "Very nice to meet you, Penny. My name is Ernest T. Bottomwhite."

"That's a funny name," she says with a slight giggle.

"Who are you talking to?" the girl's mother asks as she enters the room.

"Ernest Bottomwiggle."

I hate to interject, but I must. "It's Bottomwhite."

"I mean Bottomwhite."

"Well, that is quite the unusual name. Are you ready to go? We could stop and get some ice cream before we head home."

"No!" I shout. Where are my manners? "Please excuse my outburst. I'm enjoying our chat. I don't want you to leave. Will you be returning to the house? I'd like to chat more."

"Ernest likes to talk to me. He wants to know if we are coming back."

The woman sits on the other side of her daughter and takes her hand. I have the strangest feeling that this girl has seen other ghosts in her brief life.

"I have to return next week after they finish the grand parlor. Would you like to come with me again?" the woman asks.

"Yes, please," Penny says to her mother, then turns toward me. "See you next week."

Penny and her mother leave Annesdale holding hands. My mind races. What do I want to say to the girl? How do I tell her my story? I finally have something to look forward to.

❧

Six days later, on June 27, 2016, workers find my remains inside a previously sealed fireplace along with a metal pendant of Saint Dominic. The workers do not touch anything and neither do the two police officers that arrive a few hours later. They do not seem concerned. My bones are old and delicate, and the police aren't even sure if the remains are human. Where is Penny when I need her? I need to tell her my story. I'm afraid if the police remove my bones, I will cease to be a ghost. Luckily, the police do not consider this a crime scene. They put up yellow tape and advise the owner that someone will return in the next few days to gather the bones. Now, it's a waiting game. Will Penny return in time?

❧

The following day, at ten o'clock in the morning, Penny and her mother arrive. I want to rush over and give the little girl a hug, but it's something I cannot do.

"Good morning, Penny," I say. "Is it possible to have a chat with you and your mother in the sunroom?"

Today, Penny is carrying a pink stuffed bunny. She smiles and tugs on her mother's shirt. "Ernest is here and wants to talk to us."

The woman squats down to be eye level with her daughter. "Tell Ernest I must take some pictures first. I'll meet you in the sunroom."

Penny hugs her mom. "Ernest can hear you, mommy. You just

can't hear him. Remember?"

The woman nods and stands. "My apologies, Ernest. I'll see you in fifteen minutes."

As the woman walks away, Penny says, "Mommy took me to the doctor again yesterday. She's worried about me. About seeing ghosts. The doctor says I'll grow out of this phase. They don't understand."

We walk in silence to the sunroom. I feel bad for Penny. For being misunderstood. The same thing happened to me. People misunderstood me and I ran away from home at fifteen.

We sit in the same chairs as last week. "What is your bunny's name?" I ask.

"Ernest, of course," she says as though I should have known.

I'm torn between feeling honored and sad. "Did the doctor give you the bunny?"

"Yes." Penny sets the bunny on the chair next to her. "I also have a blue bear and a brown kitty. But you're the only one who has talked nice to me. I like you."

Penny's words are genuine. "I like you too."

Penny's mother walks in the room and is about to sit on me when Penny says, "Next chair, mommy. Don't sit on Ernest."

The woman obliges and sits in the chair to my left. "What is it Ernest wants to tell me?"

I say, "Tell her to get a pad and pencil and write down what I tell you."

Penny relays the message, and the woman pulls out a notepad and pen.

At first, the woman is skeptical. She is writing my message, but I feel it is only an exercise to appease her daughter. But soon her facial expressions change. I believe she knows her daughter is saying words that she doesn't understand, and I feel she's slowly believing in ghosts. Over the next thirty minutes, I tell my story, a few words at a time to Penny, who recites the words to her mother. It is a slow process, but I feel a great burden being lifted off my shoulders when I finish.

"Ask your mother if she will kindly read back the story. For accuracy," I say to Penny.

"Mommy, will you please read the story to Ernest? Something about accuracy."

The woman smiles and clears her throat. "I hated to leave Rebecca, but it was my duty to join the confederate army. In my first week, I was shot in the arm and ended up at Annesdale, which had been turned into a hospital during the war. Even with a bad arm, I stood guard during the night. By the third night, everyone but a dying man in a bed upstairs had left. A crying woman barged in at two in the morning, demanding to see a doctor. Her child was not breathing. I could not help her, and she took out her anger on me, shooting me and dragging my lifeless body into the fireplace, where she set me on fire. Over three weeks went by before soldiers entered Annesdale again. They quickly sealed off the fireplaces, and my remains went unnoticed until yesterday. I need you to find Rebecca Bottomwhite's family and tell them that I loved Rebecca, my only love, and did not walk away from her."

A sense of satisfaction washes over me as the woman has accurately penned my story. My only hope is that she will follow up and find any ancestors and let them know I didn't abandon my sweet Rebecca.

Penny is now twelve years old and having to research her family genealogy for a school project. She finds the assignment fascinating and on a sunny September Saturday, she and her mother visit the genealogy center at the local library. It is in a folder labeled *Tinsdale*, inside a box tucked behind the microfilm reader, that she finds a letter that changes her life.

"Mom!" she yells. "You are never going to believe this!"

"Indoor voice, Penny," her mother scolds her in a hushed tone.

Penny cannot control her excitement. She waves the paper in front of her mother's face. "Ernest Bottomwhite. Do you remember? I forgot all about him until now. He was my friend from that big house. You took pictures, and you wrote down his story. I made you type it and read it to me every night for like a year. He's related to us!"

"Slow down, Penny. What did you find?"

"It's a letter written by my great-great-great grandmother Rebecca. Her daughter Penny, who I'm named after, is Ernest's daughter."

"But Rebecca's last name was Tinsdale, not Bottomwhite. Look at the chart."

"Hear me out. Rebecca was married to Ernest, and he never returned from the war. She was already pregnant when she married Thomas Tinsdale. That's why we are having such a hard time with the dates not jiving. We knew Rebecca and Thomas had married quickly. Now we know why. Read this."

The battle is over, but my love has not yet returned. I fear he died during the fighting. I spoke to his commanding officer this afternoon. It was an unpleasant meeting. The man's behavior was disrespectful and aggravating. He claimed not to have known my dear Ernest at first. When he found I would not go away, he told me Ernest abandoned his post. He'd last seen him at the hospital, being treated for a minor gunshot wound to his left arm. Deep in my heart, I know Ernest would not abandon the army or me. A terrible fate intervened. I pray he held onto the Saint Dominic pendant I gave him before he left and knew I was with him at the end of his life. It breaks my heart he never got the chance to know his daughter. I'm going to name her Penny, after Ernest's grandmother.

Rebecca Bottomwhite

DOLLY'S FATE
Doyne Phillips

In 1863, at the time of the Battle of Collierville, Dean Callahan was a 16-year-old Wisconsin transplant in the western TN town. Made so by his parents Thomas and Mary Callahan in late 1853 when he was just six years old. Their move from Wisconsin was sudden and unexpected due to the loss of Mr. Thomas's business, a dry goods store lost by fire. The Callahans happened to have relatives in the area who were willing to assist them in making the move to this new community.

The relatives helped the Callahans by assisting them in finding a home and eventually a business which they were able to purchase. The local livery stable was available after the death of the owner. It was a natural fit for him and the family. Thomas was quick to involve the entire family in the business. Mary worked with Thomas in the office and of course young Dean, a lover of animals, cared for the horses. Dean became efficient with the animals. Locals came to consider him an expert.

Young Dean was aware there were differences between Wisconsin and Tennessee. He quickly caught the difference in accents. He had to listen closely and at times get explanations as to what was said. Over time he became aware of other things. Politics was new to him, especially the talk of States Rights and war. He had never heard these things in Wisconsin.

He was also introduced to the prejudices of the South. He learned how local people felt about anyone different from themselves. He was taken aback when he realized in the middle of all these political ideas, his family were thought to be Yankee Sympathizers. These feelings became more evident as tempers and differences between the Northern and Southern States grew. At the livery stable they were losing business because of it. Customers, if upset with Dean or Thomas, would be quick to refer to them as such. This grew worse as the country moved closer to war.

In the Spring of 1861 Dean was 14 years old. That spring the word came that on April 12th Fort Sumter at Charleston South Carolina was attacked by Confederate Forces, and within 34 hours the Union forces surrendered. Although there had been other minor skirmishes prior to this event, this marked the beginning of the Civil War between the States. The quick victory also gave the South expectations of a quick and victorious war. A notion they would soon realize was false.

The town continued to hear of other battles far away in the East. They were 1,000 miles from here and it seemed only to be tales from afar. Many of the men in town had expectations of going East to join forces and left to do so. Little did they know the battle would soon be coming to them.

In June of 1862 Dean was 15 years old when he and the town of Collierville got the news of the Naval Battle of Memphis on the Mississippi River, some 35 miles to the west. The Naval Battle, just north of Memphis, was watched by many Memphis citizens from the bank of the Mississippi River. These citizens witnessed a crushing defeat and a nearly total eradication of the Confederate

Navy. The Confederate Navy went into battle with eight Ram boats. Seven of them were destroyed or captured, 100 sailors killed or wounded, and 150 captured. The U.S. Navy had gone into battle with five Ironclad boats and four Rams. One Ram was disabled, and one sailor wounded. This brought to light the significance of professionally trained commanders as opposed to civilian commanders with no prior military experience. This news brought the war close to home for Dean and his family. It also made the realization of the possibility of the South losing the war real.

The Naval loss in Memphis allowed the movement of Union troops into western Tennessee. They set up occupation of the city of Memphis and there they established a prison to hold the many Confederate soldiers captured in the various battles. There were also regiments of Union troops occupying various smaller towns around, one of which was in Germantown, Tennessee just five miles from Collierville.

On October 11, 1863, with Union and Confederate troops operating in Western Tennessee and Northern Mississippi, Union Mag. General William T Sherman decided to leave Memphis heading east for what would become his March to the Sea. His first stop would be Collierville, TN. There he would have available to him a garrison of some 480 infantry men who had established defenses at the railroad depot, which was one block north of the Callahan's Livery Stable, and a stockade with a wall eight feet high and a line of rifle pits.

Also operating in the area was Confederate Brig. General James R. Chalmers. Chalmers was commanding a calvary of 3,000 men composed of soldiers from Tennessee, Mississippi and Missouri. Chalmers had two Big Guns, a six and a ten pound, and four rapid fire Williams Guns. Chalmers was based about 60 miles away from Collierville in Oxford, MS and had information of Mag General Sherman's movement toward Collierville. Chalmers began his move toward Collierville as well.

Chalmers had planned attacks from the south, east and north. The south was to take the depot, the east was to attack the stockade and those from the north would come in and capture the town and stockade. His forces from the north were delayed due to capturing a large camp of Union Calvary. They took 150 prisoners along with 18 wagons of supplies and destroyed an additional 30 wagons. A great success, but this delayed the attack from the north on the stockade. His forces from the east and south attacked the train, depot and stockade. Chalmer's forces forced all the Union troops into the depot, stockade and railroad cuts. They forced Mag. General Sherman and his troops to abandon the train as well and retreat to the stockade. Without his forces from the north side of Collierville, Chalmer's remaining forces could not overcome the Union forces. The delay of those forces and the risk of Union reinforcements coming from Germantown five miles away was enough for Chalmers to decide to withdraw. He did so without capturing the Union troops and Mag. General Sherman.

The losses for Chalmer's forces were 51 men killed or wounded while Union losses were 18 dead and 80 wounded or missing. Sherman narrowly escaped capture, which leaves all to only guess what effect that might have had on the war. The Union troops fleeing the train to the stockade and depot left the train open for the Confederate troops to board and capture Sherman's personal items as well as his horse Dolly.

Dolly was captured in the middle of battle. The train, being near the Callahan's Livery, was the immediate choice for holding Dolly. She was rushed there for safekeeping until something could be decided in battle. Dean was entrusted with the care of Dolly until further notice. He couldn't have been more honored to care for a general's horse, even if it was a Union General's horse.

To Dean, Dolly was a beauty. Although it was said she was one of Sherman's five horses, Dean couldn't imagine any of the others being more beautiful than Dolly. Dean had her for only a short period of time, but it was long enough to make a connection. He realized her importance when there was a guard set watch over them both. Once it was determined the Confederate forces would be retreating, Dean knew they would be taking Dolly with them. After all it would be a great trophy and give them bragging rights.

Dean found out later when General Sherman was asked about

losing his horse Dolly, he had said she was one of his least favorite of the five horses he had. He went on to state she was very temperamental. Dean was not deterred. He knew Dolly and knew she was exceptional! After all, if you had been embarrassed as the general was, what would you say?

Soon the word had spread of the captured horse Dolly and Dean being the caretaker. People came from far and wide to see the stall where General Sherman's Dolly was kept. They also wanted to meet Dean and hear more from him on the matter. Happenstance had come calling on the Callahan family and it was a welcome visitor. No more were they seen as Yankee Sympathizers but as heroes.

Dean never heard from the Confederate forces again or of the fate of Dolly. He was content to think others saw her beauty as he had and were taking good care of her.

A DAY AT THE MEMPHIS BOTANICAL GARDENS
Jan Wertz

We are the two bronze cranes in the formal gardens of the Memphis Botanical Gardens. Together, in the shifting shadows of the Sensory Garden, we watch the fish swimming in the statuary pond we stand in. There's pond flora at our feet, and a frog who pops up at unexpected moments. This area includes tall wooden shade elements, where the carpenter bees bore their homes, and leave to find the nectar in the garden's seasonal flowers.

This is the area some people come to as a place to sit and think, while they enjoy the cool shade, and the perfume of the current floral offerings. Butterflies dance on fingers of sunlight. However, the old fashioned park bench we cranes can barely see in among the perfectly trimmed hedges has no person or creature enjoying the breezes. The holly bush beside that bench is where Mama Mockingbird has her nest. I can hear the high pitched cheeps of her young begging for food. Any human, child or adult, who either tries sitting on the Mockingbird Bench, or, heaven help them, tries to look into her nest to see the babies, faces the wrath of Mama! She takes no prisoners! She does take sharp diving squawking pecks at any being too close to her nest, sometimes getting bits of someone's hair to the chorus of their surprised cries!

Occasionally there is a bit of excitement. A pair of young people come in to look around. She turns her back for a moment to look at a butterfly, or to keep an eye out for Mama. When she turns back around, she finds her date on one knee, a hand offering her a small open box, a sparkle inside... Surprised, her hand goes to her mouth. "Oh!" The cranes are always curious about the girl's reply. Some say, "Oh! Yes, I will..!" A few say something like, "Oh! I can't. Not yet... It's just too soon."

And then there was That Time... Tall Crane looks at Fishing Crane. They both burst out laughing! No forgetting that one! It only happened once, but, Wow! He was being the hopeful suitor, she had just seen the Little Box, when Another Girl arrived! 'Angry' didn't describe her adequately. "Tony! Not again?!" Tony's mouth dropped, his fingers dropped The Box, and he bolted like an Olympic sprinter, clearing the hurdle of the hedge, then the outer wall, and out into the parking lot. He didn't slow down.

The first girl was standing in shock, not believing what had just happened. The second girl, hands on hips, looked over at her, saying, "If I were you, I'd leave that ring right here. If you wear it, your finger could turn green. You're my brother's second fiancé this week." Then, turning on her heel, she walked away; her anger was for the departed Romeo, not the latest Juliet.

The fishing crane laughed, saying, "She took that ring out of the box, and put it on your beak! I wonder if it's still in the Lost & Found box in the office."

"That's almost as bad as the winter day the kingfisher landed on my wing, and used it for a diving board as he fished for some of our little pond sickleback fish." The two bronze birds enjoyed a chuckle at their memories before today broke in on them again.

A couple of teenaged girls, sans dates, came giggling in. Their make-up done to the nines, with the latest perfume on, they were trying to look like super models, but seemed more like kewpie dolls. Moments later, they dashed out shrieking, pursued by a wasp, and a couple of big carpenter bees. Shiny black abdomens catching the sun, the bees joined the wasp in following the sweet floral scent of the girls' over applied perfumes. Who ever said the gardens were boring? Not the cranes!

I'm the bright red Oriental Bridge. I was built to be part of the Memphis in May Celebration the year Japan was honored. Japanese girl drummers danced on my arch as they beat out their percussive dance tunes. Now, I'm a favorite place for taking photos of family and friends. Off to one side is another, entirely different bridge made of walking stones set into the narrow portion of the pond, just where it transitions into a swampy area. The colorful koi carp, the giant cousins of little home aquarium goldfish, swim around, sometimes under my span, in hope the walkers will use the fish pellet dispenser. One spring day, an older man, who seemed a bit sad, and his adult daughter came to take just such a photo. Seeing the fish, the man bought some of the feeding pellets, and tossed some to the koi. The landing spot became a solid mass of the wriggling colorful fish, their marbled colors flashing in the sun as they competed for the kibble treats. Another offering brought even more fish, and a smile to the man's face, as if the sun had come out from behind a cloud.

In the pond, Canadian geese proudly parade their new goslings. The gander keeps an eye out for any threat, or visitor bringing bits of bread.

The area beyond the bridge is a montage of colors. The azaleas are in bloom, providing bright pinks, coral, and white blooms. Off on one end, there is an area given over to daffodils. A bride-to-soon-be and her photographer have no trouble finding places suitable for pictures. They began with the cherry blossoms, the trees looking like pale pink sweet scented clouds. Now, the almost bride poses, seated on a plastic tablecloth to protect her white gown, the daffodils contrasting in color and texture with her face. The telephoto lens has the yellow blooms behind her go from almost in focus, to soft blurs behind her. This is the photo she will use to send out to family members who won't be able to attend the wedding. With no shortage of floral backgrounds, the photo shoot is a guaranteed success. The bride's sunny smile tells the tale.

The sun sends long shadows as the day begins its shift into dusk and then begins to set. If there is a Concert in the Park, the musicians tune up, their musical notes floating in the darkening sky, as the stars come out to listen. The daytime people visiting the garden depart, turning the Garden over to the evening's visitors and other creatures of the night. Raccoons come out. Some hunt for crayfish in the shallows of the swamp and forest area near the koi pond and bridge. A possum carries her young ones on her back as she hunts the forest litter for the insects, and other small creatures on her menu. Bats appear, hunting for flying insects. The streetlights near the fence bordering the parking area and streets attract plenty of bugs for their supper. The garden never actually sleeps; the creatures of the day shift are traded for the night shift. A fox hunts among the Azaleas for mice; the geese sleep in a watchful group to keep their fuzzy gray goslings safe.

A coyote, who lives across the street on the grounds of the art museum, comes to see if he might find an incautious small rabbit for his evening meal. The fox knows about him, but isn't worried. A gray fox, he can always climb up in a tree, then taunt his competing enemy in safety. Just another day at the garden. The night will end with the first fingers of the sun's light as the birds' dawn chorus announces the new day, beginning the pattern again. With time, the seasons also follow suit, spring following the deepest cold of winter.

HERE LIES
Judy Creekmore

I'd just returned from Elmwood Cemetery when Cissy came to tell me I had a visitor waiting on the front porch. I set my gardening tools on the back steps and put on a welcoming smile.

"You knew my uncle, Caldo Iacobello," she said without preamble.

The woman with the heavy Italian accent was late in coming. I'd expected a visit ten years ago.

"Probably better than anyone alive." I stepped aside, opening the door wide. "Please come in."

Cissy, our housekeeper for the past 40-plus years, said she would bring iced tea. I knew she'd want to show off. There'd be a plate of cookies and small cakes enough for a dozen guests.

Angela Rapisarda followed me into the den and waited for me to indicate where she should sit. Once settled, she leaned forward. "I saw Caldo's obituary. Please tell me all you know of him."

I nodded and held up a hand to indicate I'd need a minute to decide where to start.

"For a while Joe, as he was known to my family, came frequently to collect the food Cissy put in a cloth bag and hung on the back gate for him. Most often it was a cheese sandwich, a piece of fruit, and a cookie. Sometimes I made a point to watch for him just to say hello.

"At first, Mother discouraged me. Eventually, she said I might learn a lot from a person like Joe."

It took a minute to continue my narrative. "He always made a show of looking for anyone who might overhear before starting. 'This can't go any farther,' he'd whisper. I swore it wouldn't. It was fun to pretend I was a co-conspirator. He was a good storyteller and I knew much of what he said was too outlandish to be real."

I took a sip of tea before going on. "As I grew older, it seemed he tried harder to find stories that would keep me listening longer. After each visit, Mother wanted to know all he'd said. So, for several years, this Southern Jewish Princess learned all she could from the Italian man who had had a hard life but took the time to tell a joke and tease a gawky pre-teen."

As I related these memories, Angela gave an occasional nod.

"Your uncle Caldo always looked rakish in a flat cap that he said was called a coppola cap in Sicily, and that it was a symbol of masculinity."

"Yes," she said with an impatient wave of her hand.

That flick of crimson-nailed fingers told me my cousin was not there to learn about Caldo.

The flood of memories did not stop.

Angela would never know that one day all those years ago, I had commented that Joe missed a spot shaving and suggested he needed a new razor. He said he used a straight razor he'd had since puberty; and added that he always carried it with him. He reached into the righthand pocket of his raincoat. "You see? It just needs to be stropped to bring back the edge."

Two years later, I came home one day and found Joe and Mother standing in the backyard, obviously arguing. He grabbed Mother by the arm and before I could react, her other arm swung back gaining momentum for a slap that I heard across the yard.

Joe's hand went to the right pocket of his raincoat.

I couldn't move.

Mother took a step closer to him, and their eyes locked.

I couldn't breathe, much less speak.

Then, with a tip of his cap, Joe left without a word.

Mother became aware of me. "Come, sheifale," she said holding out her hand. We sat in the gazebo for hours and had the first of many talks about her past.

"I knew Joe in Catania," she began. "He thinks I should ask your father to intercede with his business partners in Italy so they will discreetly protect the family that abandoned me." She caressed my hair. "Joe's brother's third wife was my sister. She was not even born when they sent me away.

"We owe my sister nothing. Except, your father has a soft heart and will say that we share blood and they need help."

❧

Instead of these memories, I told Angela I'd left home after college, then retired as a CPA to move back to Memphis to care for my ailing parents. I continued as if I hadn't noticed her impatience. "I recently sold the family shipping company. Since then, I've volunteered to maintain gravesites at Elmwood, a historic cemetery."

Angela checked her cell. "Scusi," she said. "I need to reply to this."

She would never hear that the last time I saw her uncle Caldo, he was dying. His cap was filthy and greasy from years of use. His relatively new raincoat had lost most of its buttons and his pants hung low on narrow hips. He smelled of stale urine.

That last time.

The man I knew as Joe removed his cap and nodded. "Miss Sarah. It's always good to see you."

"I've missed our visits," I said honestly.

He asked if I would sit on the porch and talk with him. "I may be leaving soon and want to tell someone my story before I go," he said. "It's not good to leave without a word."

Joe followed me to the house, and I called for Cissy to bring iced tea to the gazebo. He and I settled on opposite sides of a small wrought iron table. "My name is Caldo Iacobello and I come from a little place in Catania, Sicily."

"And we've been calling you Joe all these years," I said.

"It was better to be called Joe." He accepted a glass of tea from Cissy with a nod. When she left, he began again.

He said that his family owned a small farm where they grew lemons, grapes, and olives. They had lived in a limestone house surrounded by fences of volcanic rock that held their one cow and pig.

Caldo wanted a different life. He wanted to join the Cosa Nostra so good jobs in hospitals and on the docks would be available to him. His father beat him, his mother cried, and his brother said, "Go! Do not come back." And Caldo never returned.

He was one of thousands who left Sicily for the United States. The Cosa Nostra arranged for him and many others to get jobs on the docks in New Orleans. He knew that others were bound for New York and other port cities. They would earn a good wage, and pay part of it to the Mafia, as the Cosa Nostra was known.

"I misjudged Carlos Marcello, the boss in New Orleans," he said. "I did something he didn't approve. It was better to leave."

"Did you come to Memphis?"

"Not yet. I needed to get far away," he said. "I'd met a guy. Just off a boat. Convinced him we needed to go to New York and get better jobs."

Joe looked down at the ground. "We hitchhiked, jumped freight trains.

"One night we had a boxcar to ourselves—nearly to New York—and this guy was dreaming big. Talking about sending money back home to family. After he fell asleep, I did what I had to do."

"What did you have to do?"

"It took a second after he fell asleep. Then I took the little money he had and his identity papers. I jumped off the train and became Mario Coco."

"You killed Mario Coco!"

Joe shrugged. "He would not have lasted long in New York.

"I again worked on the docks. Became known as a guy who could do things. Worked my way up. Again, I misjudged."

He looked into my eyes. "Remember, never get cocky. It only takes one mistake.

"Then, I came to Memphis."

"Who did you kill this time?"

"His name was Giuseppe Grasso. I was Giuseppe Grasso for a long time. It was not a lucky name for me." He made the sign of the cross. "I hurt my back on the docks. I couldn't get my name known to the big bosses. Couldn't get a job.

"So, I became Joe Panhandler. I washed dishes, swept floors. Things a man should not have to do."

While he drank tea and ate cookies, I sat staring at my hands, not wanting to look at him.

"One day they needed a delivery guy at a piano store. I told them, 'Sure I can help carry a piano into a house.' But my back was still bad, so I planned to pretend to hurt my back as soon as I touched it. It didn't work. The boss told me that if I didn't carry the weight, I wouldn't have to worry about not getting paid for a job ever again.

"It was like a miracle. We got to the house and took in the piano. I got paid, and vowed I was through with that!"

"What did you do?"

"I kept washing dishes and sweeping floors. Then, one day, as I passed this fancy house, I saw your mother clipping roses. So the next day I struck up a conversation with a cute maid named Cecile who was out sweeping the walk. I was still a handsome guy back then. We talked a while; I told her a sob story. The next day, she left food hanging for me on the gate."

He finished the tea and wiped his mouth on a napkin. "I knew I was on to something. I connected with another maid, and so on. After a while, people would put out clothes, soap. Many things. I sold what I couldn't use, and had a little walking-around money. Bussed tables and washed dishes for a local café at night. Slept in the storeroom."

"Joe, why are you telling me this?"

"Scusi. I thought I was clear. My request is that when you hear I am dead, write an obituary and run it in the Commercial Appeal. Say, "Caldo Iacobello from Catania, Sicily is dead. He is survived by many friends like Sarah Strasser who always treated him with respect."

I leaned forward. "I might have done that for Joe Panhandler, a man I always enjoyed talking to. Someone I felt a connection with." I shook my head. "Why would I do it for a heartless murderer?"

"Because a man should not die without people knowing…"

I held up a hand. "Like Mario and Giuseppe?"

Caldo shrugged.

"Maybe someone from Catania will see my name in the obituary. There are people who look for names so they can stop planning retribution. They will say, 'He died in Memphis, Tennessee.' My brother will hear and know I am dead."

"That's not all of it," I said and waited for more.

∽

Now, ten years later, Angela Rapisarda appeared. Caldo had not mentioned her specifically, but told me there would be someone from the family and I should be aware of their motives for visiting.

Her appearance explained the feeling of being watched that I'd had for a couple of weeks. I'd never seen so many delivery trucks that didn't leave packages. There was even an electric company meter reader—our area of Memphis had changed from analog readers a few years ago, eliminating the need for someone to come to our homes.

Angela finally looked up from her phone. "Someone always knew how to find Caldo. People watch," she said.

"Why did you wait this long to contact me?"

"My father, Roberto, didn't want you to know until after his death; he was afraid you would go to him and he did not want to meet the product? Yes, the product of the shame Caldo brought upon his best friend's family."

I nodded acknowledgment.

"You are not surprised?"

I straightened my posture. "How could I not know? With every year it was more evident. I couldn't look into eyes just like mine and not suspect. I couldn't put on lipstick without being reminded of the curve of Caldo's lips and how they were placed over the same jawline as my own.

"Mother told me when she saw that it could no longer be denied. And, I did my research too after he told me his story—or the story he wanted me to know. My parents and Caldo told me many conflicting versions of their lives."

I was afraid the sigh that escaped my lips betrayed my feelings. Angela did not appear to notice. "I've waited so long to hear from my Italian family. Why are you here now?"

My cousin took a minute to frame her thoughts. "Your mother—she was christened Maria—was 16 and wanted to go with Caldo on the ship, but her family said 'no.' That was before they knew she was pregnant. They kept her from him."

I nodded and took up the story from there.

"My mother had a daughter and no husband, so they sent her with a family to the US. She pretended to be a widow and soon got a job as a maid in a wealthy home. She worked hard there for four years, then met a young Jewish man. They married. She changed her name and her religion when they moved to Memphis. There were more business opportunities for him here. He became known. They became wealthy. They bought this house."

Angela looked around the room.

"What about your family?" I asked.

She stood. "*My* family prospered despite not joining the Mafia," she said. "My grandfather and father bought land when the others left. We expanded our farm, built a winery, and now ship our products to markets around the world."

"But?"

"It hasn't been easy. They say the Mafia is weak now, that only 10-15 percent of Corleone is Mafia-run," she spat. "How many does it take if their will is enforced by violence?"

Angela held her words while Cissy removed the empty tea glasses. Just able to contain herself, she continued, "My father has died. Since I speak fluent English, it was his wish for me to come to you and tell you that you own half of all he left. It was the will of my grandparents." She took a step closer to me. "*My* father grew the farm into one of the most successful in our region. We are not the poor family Caldo left behind."

"I could tell you are a woman of means," I said.

"I am a lawyer," she said proudly. "Because Caldo had been a member of the Mafia when he left Italy, I cannot practice law in my own country. In Italy, no one associated with the organization, going back five generations, is eligible to hold a job in law. So, I had to leave my home to attend an English-speaking college to earn a degree. I recently began working as a patent attorney in Washington, DC."

Angela suddenly loomed over me. "I respect my family's wishes. So, I'm here to make you an offer, *le mia cara cugina*."

This was the moment I'd dreaded for a decade.

"Angela, there is no need to haggle over the inheritance. I will freely, and with best wishes, sign it over to you," I said. "*My dear cousin*, I don't want to become someone other than who I am. I want to remain Sarah Strasser, a woman of leisure in Memphis."

The lawyer's thick false eyelashes shielded her eyes.

I stood, forcing her to step back. My gaze took in every corner of the comfortable room, then the lush garden on view through a wall of windows. "Why would *I* want more?" I stepped over to Cissy and placed my arm through hers. "It would only complicate my life."

With a slight nod, Angela smiled. "My family thanks you. We'll send you a case of wine."

"I have connections at Graceland if you'd like a private tour while you're here," I countered.

Both offers were declined.

We tried visiting as cousins, tactfully phrasing our inquiries to each other. We soon gave up the effort, and I was happy to see a black limousine with tinted windows appear just as we reached the front gate. We swapped air kisses and said we'd keep in touch while the chauffeur held open the car door.

Cissy, my life-long protector, waited for me on the porch.

"Do you think I just dodged a bullet—or a straight razor?" I asked, my heart racing.

"Oh, sugar, I think she bought the whole, 'Why would I want more?' line."

"I had ten years to get it right!" I said, and sat on the top step.

"You should have told her you already have a warehouse full of her olive oil, limoncello, and wine," Cissy chided and kneaded my shoulders.

The next morning, I returned to Elmwood Cemetery to finish weeding and watering the flowerbed around my mother and father's monument. I thanked them for being wonderful parents.

On the other side of the cemetery, I tidied flowers I'd planted on Caldo's grave. I thanked him for giving me life, and sharing some things my parents hadn't. He told me of deals my father made with the Sicilian Mafia to help the Iacobello family prosper; and that Uncle Robert was only too happy to work for, if not join, them. It was also good to know that his brother had carried a straight razor.

"Dad, I met Uncle Roberto's daughter Angela yesterday. She stood over me like a bird of prey eying a field mouse. 'I'm here to make you an offer, *le mia cara cugina*,' she said.

"I almost asked, 'And whose family do you think has been protecting yours, enabling it to grow all these years?' I think it's better that she not know."

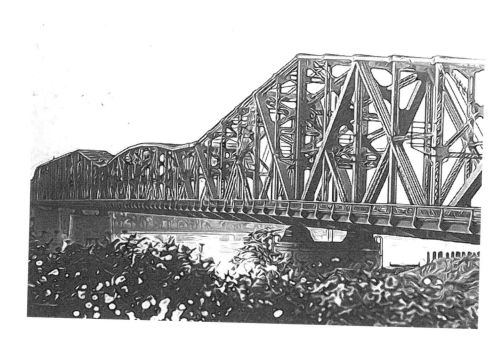

THE BULLET IN MY POCKET
Steve Bradshaw

"What happened to 'em'?" The corpulent homicide detective asked, pinching his nose.

Ben Morgan ignored the premature question as he felt the neck and inched up the back of the head for trauma. His latex fingertips moved through graying bushy hair and scalp, forehead, temples, and then forced open eyelids—*no way...*

"Who is this man?" he huffed, his penlight in a socket. "Who found him, and a time?"

With a hard swallow the detective kept his nose in a puny river breeze and eyed his notepad. "Jake Holt found 'em at 2 a.m. The deceased is a Theodore Davenport."

"Theodore... Davenport...," Morgan breathed. *What're you doing down here,* he thought.

"Mr. Holt said he was night fishin'. What happened to his eyes, Doc?"

"They're missing," Morgan barked. "Holt the suspicious type?"

Stacey cocked his head in the breeze. "Gut says not involved, but it's still early."

Dr. Benjamin Morgan looked more like a retired school bus driver than skilled forensic pathologist and the Shelby County Chief Medical Examiner. His wiry stature, curled posture, sunken chest, and bald head were unfortunate family traits. His high IQ was a gift he never wanted. His attitude came from working nights with dead people.

He gave up on humanity the day Melba died, pancreatic cancer, too young and before children. No siblings. Parents long gone. Morgan was left with the dog Melba forced on him; it got hit by a dump truck the day he buried her. That night he put the dog out of its misery with Melba's .38 caliber revolver and one of the only two bullets in the cylinder.

He woke up the next day on Melba's grave holding her gun. He decided then to carry the last bullet in his pocket. When the time was right it was his ticket to Melba and escape from a world he has grown to dislike.

"Hold my penlight," he puffed as he pried open the jaw. "Nothing in there except a swollen tongue." He felt the stiff neck and rock-hard deltoids. "You know not to say anything about the eyes, right Stacey?"

"Not a word, Doc. You're the boss."

"Don't even put it in your report." From haunches he surveyed the edge of the river and wide, barren bank leading to the mound and body. "You come across any eyeballs out there?"

Stacey stammered, aghast at the thought.

"I'll take that as a hard no."

"CSI's pullin' up. They'll comb the place, some quality forensic technique, Doc."

They won't find them either, Morgan thought as he reexamined the eye sockets. *No sign of extraction; how is that even possible?*

A screeching whine eked out of the underbelly of the bridge. "You hear that?"

"All I hear is a river, Doc."

"Did you find any disturbances on this dirt mound around the body?"

"Only us. No dirt on his shoes. Like the others, he dropped outta' the sky."

"And it has not rained going on three months."

"River's way down—record lows. You think they took the-leap or got pushed?"

"An Olympian with a stiff wind couldn't get out this far, Stacey. I want you to call Cadden Reinhold. Tell him we need to talk."

"Thought you didn't like that guy. You called him a paranormal *nut-mare*."

"You're right. I don't like him, but this makes five dead. I need to consider everything."

Stacey left to call. Morgan seized the moment to study the body closer with his penlight, magnifying glass, and no lame questions.

Okay, talk to me Davenport. You're a forty-year-old, healthy male with no trauma from the fall or attack. You did not jump. You're a strong guy; coulda' fought for your life, but no defense wounds. Clothes pristine. I need you under my lights. Get my toxicology and chem screens to rule out poisons and organ failures. Sudden death with no clues—

"Hey Doc, Reinhold will meet you at sunrise. Said he knows where. Told him we found another under the Harahan."

"Help me roll 'em. Hold my penlight on the back of his head. Looking for trace blood."

A diversion. Morgan did not want Stacey to see the back of the neck. Morgan wanted to confirm presence or absence of the mark he found on the others.

"Nope. No blood, Doc," he puffed. "You any closer to tellin' me how this one died?"

"You can transport. I've got all I can get at this death scene."

Stacey signaled. Lights dribbled down the black bluff wall.

Here comes a stretcher, crash bag, and forensic suitcases, Morgan thought as he popped off his surgical gloves and perused the Harahan Bridge. The steel girders creaked and whined like some mythical iron creature awakening in a primordial Mississippi River Valley.

"You gonna answer my question, Doc?"

"No. Cause and manner, undetermined. I won't know more until the autopsy and CSI finds me something new. This will very likely join the other four cold cases…"

He parked on the oily gravel by the tracks behind the only car. The new sun hit the back of his head. The dark Harahan Bridge loomed ahead.

I wonder how long you've been here, Cadden? Morgan felt Reinhold's cold hood and elbowed into the tangled woods a hundred feet above the river. *How do temperatures around here drop so much and so fast?*

He bulldozed the brittle, dead remnants of the winter foliage and slowly descended the wall of the bluff onto an unusually wide, desolate riverbank. Still hidden from the sun, the river mist climbed everything except the Harahan.

He saw him sitting on a boulder under the bridge, the darkest shadow. Morgan approached Reinhold from behind. *This is very weird... It's like you belong here.*

"I'm very busy," he grumbled as he entered the penumbra of the bridge. His eyes jumped from the untidy fire back to the old man dressed in black—trousers, shirt, boots, long leather coat, and black felt fedora with his infamous silver dollar hat band.

Cadden Reinhold poked a stick into the hot coals like an arson toying with his demons. "We meet again," he chirped. "Don't you just hate being lost, Benjamin?" He pointed his smoking stick at a boulder. "Pull up a rock, forensic man. I think we have some time before all hell breaks loose."

"So, let's not waste any of it," Morgan pounced. "I just completed autopsy number five; another found under this bridge. Cause and manner, unknown. This must be resolved. As Chief Medical Examiner, I look at all possibilities. Facts are my tools."

Reinhold smiled as he took in the dark underbelly of the Harahan, the superstructure that spanned the Mississippi River for more than a hundred years. "Facts matter... Do you know this beauty is 4,973 feet long and 108 feet above the august body of water that divides our land?"

"Wow. That is amazing, Reinhold. Thanks for sharing." He had second thoughts about pulling up a rock.

"The Harahan Bridge opened on July 14, 1916. Do you know this construction project was so big that it took three steel companies—"

"—to complete. I really don't care."

"Officially, twenty-three workers died. Nine fell into the concrete slurry as these massive piers were poured. An awful way to go, don't you agree?"

Morgan's eyes reluctantly climbed a pier. "Yes. It would be."

"During the Great Depression seventy jumped off this bridge, most were lost in the thousands of acres of muddy water that slides by every second of every day. No tellin' how many have used the Harahan that way—"

Reinhold lit a small cigar and squinted at the sun now touching Arkansas.

"Why're you telling me this?" Morgan seethed. "Do you enjoy rehashing depressing local history, or is it just the wasting of my time?

"I have an active serial killer. I asked you to meet because I need to know more about the urban legend you tout all across the country. Who is the keeper of the Harahan Bridge, and who is the Alastor?"

"You want to know about the Alastor?" Reinhold gushed. "But wait, you don't believe; you're a genius, right? Not some charlatan apostle of Greek mythology, demonology, and urban legend. You're the perfectly-informed, the original *I-am-smarter-than-you* man."

Morgan grimaced. "Okay, I deserve that… but now our city is faced with a certifiable monster on a killing spree under this bridge. Five died in January, Dr. Reinhold. Please, I need to understand relevant mythology to understand the Harahan Bridge urban legend that has given *sick-life* to a nobody!"

"Oh. So, it's my world that created your monster."

"Butcher. Terminator. Executioner. Call it what you will. I believe an insane fanatic is playing some role in your cockamamie urban legend."

"We are sitting on sacred grounds of the Chickasaw. This land has been violated the last century: the abominable slave trading business, the scurrilous Civil War trading post, a place where detestable river pirates gather, the birthplace of the Ku Klux Klan, and burial grounds—"

"—for tens of thousands of yellow-fever victims," Morgan spewed. "I am sure the evil wrought upon these hallowed grounds shall linger for an eternity, but—"

"We are sitting at the epicenter of horrific karma!"

Morgan turned to the river; his science was not helping. He had kept the most bizarre findings under wraps: missing eyeballs with no sign of extraction, odd burn marks on backs of necks, snow-white tips of each hair strand, and something so chilling he dares not share.

A Medical Examiner reports medical-legal findings. Rulings on cause and manner of death are public record; reputations are at stake. Morgan is quoted daily in the *Commercial Appeal,* his exact words taken from official pathology reports.

He has bought time hiding behind medical terminology. *Idiopathic cardiomyopathy* is a powerful nonanswer. It sounds important but simply means hearts of five stopped for unknown reasons. A sinister killer is loose. Only Dr. Morgan is in a position to stop it.

Cadden Reinhold's unorthodox services are well known. Over three decades he's traveled five continents and purged sacred structures of demons, devils, and manifestations of the wicked departed. Although his skills are provocative, his results are profound.

The retired eighty-year-old recluse lives alone at the Peabody Hotel. Morgan has publicly excoriated the midsouthern ghostbuster, accusing him of taking advantage of the uninformed, the superstitious, and the just plain dumb. The time has come for Benjamin Morgan to put Melba's last .38 caliber bullet in his head, or to lift paranormal rocks and find some way to stop the most dangerous, phantom serial killer in Memphis history.

"You would not call unless you were forensically challenged," Reinhold quipped. "What do you have, Benjamin?"

"Another forty-year-old male found dead under the Harahan at 2:00 a.m."

"Time of death was 9:00 p.m.," Reinhold mumbled.

"Yes." *How do you know? That's not been released,* Morgan thought.

"No signs of trauma," he continued. "No defense wounds. Not shot, stabbed, strangled, or poisoned. No needle marks. No evidence of suffocation. No broken bones. No evidence of anyone at the death scene; a twenty-foot radius around the body. Not even animals."

"They avoid it."

"No signs of convulsion, choking, disease, heart, brain, vascular—"

"Enough," Reinhold snapped.

"I'm not done with—"

"Both eyes missing. All of 'em?" Reinhold inquired.

"Yes. Who is telling—"

"Please." Reinhold waves his smoldering stick. "Each were found thirty feet from the south edge of the bridge. Always east side of the river and centered on the same dirt mound."

"Yes." Morgan sighed.

"Your confirmation's not necessary," Reinhold scolded. "All have a circular, half-inch indentation, nickel-size, back center neck."

"Posterior aspect cervical spine—C2, C3. Slight searing of skin. Never seen skin melt."

"—runs like candle wax," Reinhold said. "No charring. This one only."

"Correct. Like his skin melted."

"He went willingly," Reinhold breathed.

"I don't know what that even means! His tissue slides will be ready tonight. I'm hopeful histology and more toxicology will shed new light on—"

"Keep tellin' yourself that, Benjamin. He's no different from the others."

"This is getting me nowhere," Morgan huffed.

"Calm down. Listen and learn. The hair change, it is just tips?"

"Yes. I see it with all. Seems to continue postmortem."

"You bring me pictures of them?"

Morgan passed his cellphone. Reinhold slowly scrolled and passed it back. "Okay. Nothing's gonna happen for a while. I need time to think."

"I need answers now," Morgan barked. "You either know something or you don't."

"Tell me names. I have Theodore Davenport."

"Teddy Pulley, Theo Carlson, J.T. Weser, Ted Manson. Why?"

"We're dealin' with somethin' very dangerous, Benjamin, and the location complicates it further. The Harahan Bridge is a known portal; a place where spirits move between worlds."

"Good grief, Reinhold. You've gotta be kidding me. I'm screwed."

"Fine. Go back to your saintly work; good luck with that." Reinhold turned to leave.

"Just tell me the problem with the names. Why did it shake you up?"

Reinhold opened his phone and held up a picture. "Does this man look familiar?"

"An older version of my five victims."

"Don't you think it a little odd five dead men look a lot alike, and the longer they sit in your cooler the more they look like this man? This is James Theodore Harahan, the bridge's namesake, born January 12, 1841, died January 22, 1912."

"It's January 22nd today."

"I believe this happens every January, and it will continue until it's settled."

"Until what's settled?"

"Theodore Harahan worked for the railroad; clawed his way from brakeman to President of Illinois Central Railway. He was on his way to Memphis to build this bridge when he was killed. At the time there were very hostile railroad labor union disputes. Theodore Harahan was killed in a sleeper car parked on a restricted track. They say it was a runaway train. It rammed his car! This timely death altered labor negotiations in favor of the unions."

"My God, they assassinated him!"

"Pretty obvious but never proved. Political."

"A hundred year old cold case," Morgan sighed.

"Every one of your victims has Theodore in their name. Look at your pictures; they're morphing into James Theodore Harahan's likeness."

"Assuming that is true, why are we only seeing it now? You said every January."

"The Mississippi River is at a record low, Benjamin. There is one landing spot for his victims. That dirt mound is normally underwater. In the past, the victims were lost in the river—"

"Become part of the city's 4,000+ missing persons reported every year."

"These killings will not stop until Theodore Harahan escapes the bridge's hold on him. His cold case must be solved to free his spirit. He is desperate to leave the world that ruthlessly stole his life and left that wrong unresolved."

"I cannot believe I'm listening to this crap."

"You asked me. James Theodore Harahan is the Alastor of the Harahan Bridge. Every January he avenges his wrong by taking sinful men and using their vitreous eyeballs to pass through this portal."

"The eyeballs missing. Why can't he pass?"

"There's a Cerberi, an underworld gatekeeper. It prevents *unsettled spirits* from leaving this world. Theodore Harahan is stuck in the Harahan Bridge portal."

"But why does he continue to fail?" Morgan pushes.

"I believe Theodore Harahan needs to take a sinner who knows the supernatural ropes," Reinhold boasted. "His successful passage will take someone who can outmaneuver, out play this Cerberi… someone savvy like me—"

On Reinhold's last word, a crystal-blue sphere emerges from the flickering fire; it engulfs Reinhold and expels Morgan—who is left paralyzed in the nearby river brush clutching Melba's bullet. When an inky shadow drips from the underbelly of the Harahan Bridge, Melba's bullet starts to burn Morgan's leg. Then a long rod with a sizzling-blue tip sinks into the back of Reinhold's neck. He melts, the sphere dissolves, fire dies, and Morgan falls into a dark abyss…

∾

Wearing surgical scrubs, he stands at an empty stainless-steel table. Double-doors gush open, and a naked corpse rolls into the room with folded clothes at the feet. He sees the black trousers, black shirt, black boots, and black leather coat, and the black felt fedora with the silver dollar hat band.

"Dr. Morgan," says the Director of the Memphis Police Department as he enters the room. "Cadden Reinhold is still missing. We think he fell into the river."

Confused, he stares at the hat and squeezes Melba's bullet.

"Do you know this man?" Director Melvin Shipp asks. "The eyes are missing."

His wife appears next to him. She smiles and says, "I love you, Benny." Her words and a warmth fill him like charging a battery. "You're fine, you silly man."

"Dr. Morgan," Shipp says. "I know this is a difficult time." He casually inspects a line of sterile surgical instruments neatly laid out on stainless steel counters.

"You've always liked facts," Melba whispers. "I have one for you; I'm here and God loves you very much. He told me this is your time, Benny. Only you can fix this—"

"I know you have been through a lot," Shipp rambles on as he looks into a microscope.

"God said you're ready. A little later we will be together again, Benny."

On Melba's last word, she fades away and MPD Director Melvin Shipp emerges inches from Benjamin Morgan's nose.

"I do not want to interrupt a genius at work," Shipp whispers. "I need this thing fixed, and I want you to know that you are my man. Whatever you need, no questions asked."

Melba's bullet drops to the bottom of his pocket. He places a hand on the heart of the corpse he knows—a man he had misjudged. One who now looks very different.

Dr. Benjamin Morgan turns his head and locks eyes with the second most powerful man in the city of Memphis. "First thing, we have a hundred year old cold case to solve..."

.

A PICTURE IN TIME
Annette Cole Mastron

"Nothing is impossible to a determined woman."
— Louisa Mae Alcott

Alice lays across her bed on the patchwork quilt and loudly sighs in her sun-filled bedroom.

"I heard that. Why the sigh?" her mother says, peeking her head around the doorframe.

"My essay on voting rights/women's equality is due. I don't even know where to start. I mean, let's face it. Adults all say I'm a privileged, young woman. Other than not getting paid as much as the 16-year-old male who just got hired at work in the warehouse. He knows nothing and gets more money than me. Other than that,

I don't have a real equality experience, do I?"

"Don't you? You're lying on a patchwork quilt crafted by your namesake great-grandmother, who at just a year older than you, fought the real fight for women's equity in 1920. Each square represents a piece of that fight which helps ensure your rights as an equal citizen today."

"Don't go all Equal Rights Amendment on me, Mom. It's 2024, and all is well," Alice challenges.

"Why don't you go see Miss Mary at the Cossitt Library. Ask her to show you the Memphis history room and do some actual physical research on why living in Tennessee should make you appreciate the equality legacy you benefit from today. Ask questions, open your mind, but most importantly, listen to the voices in the dusty books that hold the history."

"Really, Mom, I can just google stuff from here and go swimming later with my friends."

"Well, I guess you could take that shortcut, but if you really want to know about equality, you're going to need to do the work. Remember, not everything is on the internet. Sometimes you need a librarian. Just because you have the internet is like saying you don't need a math teacher because you have a calculator. The internet is just a tool." Thunder rumbles in the distance.

"Well fine, guess swimming is out, I might as well go to the library."

Alice throws an eye roll in her mom's direction and bends over to lace up her new tennis shoes. She grabs her backpack, stuffs her laptop in, and hustles down the stairs. Her mom dangles her keys from her pinky and says, "Be careful with my baby. If you park on the cobblestones, be sure to set the emergency brake so it doesn't roll into the river."

"No worries, Mom, I love your Z car." Alice gives her mom a cheek-peck kiss and grabs the dangling keys.

"Love you," Alice says to her mom as the backdoor shuts and her mom says, "Love you, too."

Alice starts the Z car and Taylor Swift's "Anti-Hero" is blasting out of the speakers. She grins. She loves that it is her mom's currently favorite song. It fits her perfectly.

She heads toward downtown from East Memphis traveling Walnut Grove to Union Avenue. Alice gives a hand wave to The Nineteenth Century Club mansion and takes a slight detour through Victorian Village, where the "ladies" of a different era all stand so regal and resolute, having survived each generation of progress. She passes the backside of AutoZone Park, smells the ribs from Rendezvous alley and gets a glimpse of the Peabody Hotel, known for their daily duck march to the lobby fountain. She stops at Main Street until the trolley passes and heads down the bluff to the cobblestones, dutifully applying the emergency brake as she parks.

"I can't believe the river is so busy today," Alice says to no one as she exits the car and watches the barge traffic and the tourists embarking on a riverboat tour. Alice carefully traverses the uneven cobblestones and avoids the huge metal hooks that secure barges to the riverbank. Her stomach growls and she stops at Front Street Deli for fried egg sandwiches for her and Miss Mary. She walks the block to the Cossitt Library and wonders about the 1960s "improved" design of the front of the building. To her, the front has always looked like a shiny shipping container. Before Alice's time, the front was a stunning beautiful red sandstone turreted Romanesque monument to the Victorian era. If someone looks closely enough, they can see the red sandstone foundation on the river side of the library, a testament to its 1910 origins.

As she enters the library, she's greeted by Miss Mary.

"Alice, my darling, how are you doing? Your mom said you were coming to do some research, and I've got just the spot for you. Just don't tell; not everyone gets to go to the stacks in the old part of this jewel."

"I brought your favorite from Front Street Deli. Can we eat wherever you're taking me?"

"Of course," she whispers.

She leads Alice through a maze of doors using her keycard to gain access. They go downstairs, only to then go upstairs and arrive in the secret stacks, a loft-style room filled with what appears to be ancient documents, books and maps. On the wall is a framed, yellowed poster, depicting a woman holding a baby that reads, "Women bring all voters into the world—Let women vote."

On the east wall, is a painting called "Nashville Parade for Women's Suffrage" by Shirley Martin, depicting the historic women's parade from the state capitol to Centennial Park to promote the cause of women's suffrage. Alice smiles to herself. Her great grandmother was there on May 18, 1920, and Alice has a poster of this painting on her wall at home.

Miss Mary follows her line of sight. "Aww, your great grandmother was there. Did you know? This painting shows the diversity of women who came together in 1920 when the League was founded in Nashville. A reminder of the annual May Day suffrage parade. Suffragettes and their children marched from the Tennessee capitol downtown to the Parthenon in Centennial Park. People from all racial, religious, and ethnic groups came together to stand for the VOTES FOR WOMEN and founded the League."

"Yes, she was one of the women whose life was forever changed that year."

"Those suffragettes convened in Nashville," Miss Mary elaborates. "It was the first meeting of the League of Women Voters. At that time, thirty-five states had already ratified the 19th Amendment giving women the right to vote. Anne Dallas Dudley, a Nashville suffragette as vice-president of the National Suffrage Association, addressed the "Victory Banquet" with a passionate call for Tennessee to become the thirty-sixth state. If successful, it would position the amendment to pass for women in all states to become voting citizens."

"How do you have this painting in the stacks of this old library? I thought it was on display in the Tennessee State Museum?"

"It's a secret, Alice," Miss Mary whispers. "The one in the museum is one of two. I have the first attempt, which was given to me by the artist.".

Alice looks at her, thinking that maybe she has a lot to learn at the library after all, and says, "Let's eat our sandwiches before they get cold."

"Great plan, I have the perfect spot."

Miss Mary leads Alice to the west wall of the stacks to a huge window overlooking the river and the barge traffic. There is a scarred oak bar top under the windows.

"I can't believe how busy the river is today." Alice says as she unwraps her sandwich and passes Miss Mary her packaged sandwich.

"A hundred years ago it was busier, if you can imagine. Memphis was a rough river town in those times. The archives are full of stories that depict life in Memphis at that time. In those days, men controlled every aspect of life. Women were not allowed to work outside the home." Miss Mary bites into her sandwich and lets out a sigh of approval.

"Ironically," she continues, "the first public library on this site was finished being built by the daughters of Mr. Cossitt. He died and his will didn't make provisions for finishing it, but his daughters honored his commitment to the project."

"Why, ironically?"

Miss Mary puts down her sandwich and explains, "It's ironic because only white men could be in the building. Women would need to be accompanied by a man and still couldn't check out a book. It was a gorgeous building when built and changed the skyline of Memphis. Its red sandstone exterior signaled Memphis had arrived as a cultural city, even though the city dump was located next door. Thankfully, it was relocated off the riverfront. The front of the library was angled on the block and had lovely turrets that allowed men to watch the river and monitor the arrival on their boats so they could then exit the back of the building to cross Riverside Drive and tend to their business on the river. We are now in the original part of the building; some floors are usable like this one, but others have been abandoned and left to time."

"Women couldn't check out books?" Alice exclaims.

"You know the Nineteenth Century Club on Union?" Miss Mary asks, and Alice nods.

"Your Mom and I are legacy members of The Nineteenth Century Club because of their history of good work. One of the first projects was raising funds to buy books for this very library. The Cossitt sisters made sure after their father died to complete his commitment to the city. This was a time when the oldest son would have controlled the estate assets, but these sisters made sure to finish what their father started. They were also members of the Nineteenth Century Club. They used their father's inheritance to complete the building. Then, the Nineteenth Century Club held a musical benefit to raise money to supply the new library with books.

"However, as women, they couldn't even check out the books they supplied. They developed a 'work around' through the Nineteenth Century Club and created a library at their location at 1433 Union Avenue, which was the first branch of the public library where women could check out a book." Miss Mary reminisces, staring out the river as she finishes her sandwich.

She turns to Alice with sparkling eyes and says, "Are you ready for an adventure?"

Alice searches her face and notices the photograph in her wrinkled hands. Miss Mary hands the photograph to her as she explains, "This was the Cossitt library when it was built. A beauty. We need to stand in the southwest corner of the building, each holding the yellowed library photograph. I did this with your mom and grandmother back in the day when we discovered the portal into another time."

"Do you have a hidden camera? I'm just here to do research." Alice says, not wanting to upset her.

"I'm not crazy, just come with me on the adventure of a lifetime. Sometimes, you need to go back in history to understand the present. You have a unique opportunity."

"I'm game, let's go." Alice says excitedly, as lightning flashes over the Mississippi River.

Miss Mary clasps Alice's hand and they walk to the southwest corner of the room. As they both hold the picture, Alice takes note of the steamboat in the image, just as the world begins to swirl, and she squeezes Miss Mary's hand. The swirling stops and they fall on something soft, a bed. When Alice opens her eyes, Miss Mary is young and dressed in a costume of some sort.

"Miss Mary?" Alice asks tentatively.

"Shush, we have to get you dressed, and I'm just Mary."

She rummages through a trunk at the end of the bed, throwing clothes onto the bed. "Quick, your great great grandmother Verna will be coming through that door in 10 minutes."

Alice stares blankly at her, not understanding.

"Strip," she says, and Alice does, still not grasping the situation. Miss Mary approaches her and shoves a scratchy muslin shift over her head before placing the final dress on her. The dress is yellow, not Alice's choice color but it is soft and swishes when she turns. Alice looks out the window as the floor moves and realizes she is on a boat. She glances across the river and sees the Arkansas farmland her family once owned. Her great grandmother's brother lost all their land in a bad hand of cards after a drinking marathon, thrusting her family into poverty during the Great Depression. Alice's head spins. Where are the bridges? How did they get here?

"Where are the two bridges?" she asks, voicing one of many questions swimming through her mind.

"Honey, we are back in May, 1920. When someone asks you about things, say I got it in Nashville during the suffragette meeting on May 18, 1920. You were with the Memphis suffragists group and we went by your family's steamboat to convene in Nashville for the first meeting of the League of Women Voters. You went with your best friend, me, your great great grandmother Verna, your great grandmother Alice, and your 'brother' as chaperone."

A knock at the door makes Alice jump.

"Come in," Miss Mary says. Alice's great great grandmother, Verna, enters. She knows her instantly. Her picture from the Nashville rally sits on Alice's walnut dresser back in 2024.

Verna says to Alice, "We are docked, but the carriages are not here yet. Why are you wearing that dress, your suffragette dress?"

She walks over and puts her hand on Alice's forehead while saying, "You're a sweaty mess, and Billy is coming to take us home. He would be a great husband for you. Next year, you'll need to pick. A spring wedding, I think."

Alice turns away from Verna and rolls her eyes at the husband comment. She walks out the door of the cabin and glimpses 1920 Memphis, which has virtually no skyline except for the completed Cossitt Library and the US Customs house. On the side of the library appears to be a city dump. The cobblestones are stacked three high with bales of cotton which are being loaded onto mule wagons and taken up from the river to a cotton warehouse across from the impressive library.

Verna follows Alice saying, "Go get your brother. He's supposed to be supervising the cotton offloading. What are those shoes?"

Behind Verna, Miss Mary shakes her head, no.

Alice replies as Miss Mary had instructed her. "I got them in Nashville. They match my dress." It's now that Alice realizes she is still in her modern running shoes, which thankfully have a yellow stripe down the side.

Miss Mary grabs Alice and pulls her back in the cabin, whispering urgently, "You're not supposed to interact with anyone."

"Why not? I'm going to find 'my brother.' He lost my family's fortune, and I want to see why men in the 1920s were thought to be better at business than women. Ridiculous."

"Oh boy," is all Mary can think as she trails after Alice.

Alice finds him on the upper deck drinking with Billy, her would-be suitor. "Ugh. Not in a hundred years," she thinks, suddenly grateful for the time she actually lives in. 1920 could use some modernizing.

"Gene, you're supposed to be at the cotton warehouses supervising our cotton."

Gene turns from his bourbon and says, "I knew Nashville would get you all worked up. Women should be wives, run the house and raise children. Stay in their place. Women aren't smart enough to be voters or in business."

"You really are a weak, stupid, illiterate drunk. You think women as voters are a problem, as you sit there day drinking because you're the male heir. Give me a break. You'd never survive in 2024. You're a disgrace to our family. You're incapable of conducting our family's business. Oh, by the way, Verna's looking for you and Billy."

Alice looks now at Billy, having heard this story for years. She looks in his bloodshot blue eyes and says, "Whatever deal you have with Gene, here, it's not happening. There will be no marriage to me, ever. So move on. I'm not marrying a version of this sorry excuse for a brother. You see, in a couple of years, Gene here, loses our family land and business. I'm not going to ever marry someone like him."

Verna stands, open mouthed, in the doorway, as she glances at Alice, and then at Gene and Billy. Clearly, she heard the conversation.

Alice turns toward Verna, "If you don't stop Gene he will lose everything you hold dear. I'm going up to our warehouse and I'll handle the family business."

"But how do you know what to do?" Verna asks.

"Come with me and I'll show you how to grade cotton. I've been doing it since I was in the sixth grade. I followed Dad around before he died; I know what to do. I'm not cut out to be a debutante wife. I'm sure not marrying the likes of a picked beau. The women's march in Nashville 1920 is an indication that times are changing. Hard times are coming, but I'm more concerned for our family. Come with me."

Alice takes her great great grandmother by the hand, looking over her shoulder as Billy and Gene continue to drink.

Miss Mary grasps Alice's hand with the Cossitt Library picture and says, "We have to go." Alice shakes her head determinedly, exclaiming, "I'm going to save my family, I'm staying here, in 1920."

Miss Mary tears the picture in half and tucks it into the rosette covered pocket of Alice's dress, winks, and disappears. Alice, still clutching Verna's hand, exits the steamboat onto the 1920s cobblestones into an unfamiliar Memphis at approximately the same spot where she left her Mom's Z car in 2024. Time to see what equality looks like at the beginning.

AUTHOR BIOS

BETH ALVAREZ is a prolific multi-award winning author of over two dozen young adult novels, specializing in fantasy and the paranormal. A visual arts major, she is also a freelance graphic designer who, among other things, creates all her own books covers, including *Memphis Mosaic*. Beth can be contacted via her website, where you can find her personal blog and sign up for bonus content and advance notification of new and upcoming titles. www.ithilear.com

STEVE BRADSHAW is a Forensic Investigator, Biotech Entrepreneur, Darrel Award Mystery/Thriller author and Ghostwriter with thirteen novels (softcover/eBooks) twenty shorts, and six audiobooks (Amazon Audible) available worldwide, and screenplay TERMINAL BREACH. Steve is working on his next forensic mystery/thriller The Hillsborough Nightmare series (SHARED INNOCENCE Book I now available), and KAYDA Book II releasing winter 2024. www.stevebradshawbooks.com

ANGELA BRUNSON has her PhD in Musicology and wrote her dissertation on music in the Vietnam prisoner of war camps. She also writes poetry and songs, enjoys public speaking, and loves to sing and act. She recently discovered a talent for painting and started a new career as an artist. Browse her works at AngelaBrunson.com.

JOHN BURGETTE writes in several styles, including poetry, research, sermons, and short stories. His background includes computer science, social sciences, academic research, and lay ministry. Besides contributing to several of the CC Writers' anthologies, his creative writing has appeared in *Southern Writers Magazine* and *Tennessee Magazine*.

KAREN BUSLER is a professional symphony orchestra musician (retired), writer, choir director, Bible study leader, and amateur chef. She has been a third-place winner and a finalist multiple times in *Southern Writers Magazine* Short Story competitions, and was a finalist in the 2024 Richard Wright Literary Awards for two of her short stories. Her full life includes writing, voicing/performing audiobooks, making Rosaries and jewelry, swimming, singing, studying, and hosting parties, in addition to making Italian gelatos, fancy decorated cakes, and her award-winning chili! Contact Karen at www.karenbusler.com.

BETH KREWSON CARTER received her degree from Meredith College, then went to work for Procter & Gamble. Later, while raising a family, she taught school for several years. She studied creative writing with Laura Grabowski-Cotton and has written for *Woman's World* magazine. She currently lives in Tennessee with her husband and the youngest of their three children. *Poison Root* is her second novel, *The Nest Keeper* was her debut in 2019.

JUDY CREEKMORE wrote for the *Times-Picayune* for 25 years. She is the author of *Celebrating 200 Years of River Parishes History,* and *Wartime Memories from Louisiana's River Parishes;* also two unpublished cozy mysteries. Her short fiction has appeared in various anthologies. She encourages others to write by word and example.

GARY FEARON is a writer, musician and voice artist. His published works include short stories and the books *After Abbey Road: The Solo Hits of The Beatles* and *Right Brain Writing: Creative Shortcuts for Wordsmiths.* With a background in broadcasting and production, he has written over 300 songs, jingles and morning show parodies. Visit him at www.garyfearon.com.

LARRY FITZGERALD is a retired businessman who enjoys writing Christian fiction, including romance and mystery. He is a former youth soccer coach and feels it is important to encourage Christian worldview thinking in the hearts and minds of our young adults, which is reflected in his new novel *A Dog Named Speed.* Visit him at LarryFitzgeraldAuthor.com.

RONALD LLOYD: Over the years, Ronald found himself rewriting plots in his head or jotting down an outline on scraps of paper. At sixty-six he retired to the back booth of a Burger King and began writing. He hopes you enjoy what he creates as much as he enjoys writing it.

ANNETTE COLE MASTRON started her writing career in the insurance industry working for over 35 years as an investigator, writing reports for a variety of clients. In 2012, she changed careers to work as Communications Director for *Southern Writers Magazine* and its blog, Suite T. She wrote for both the magazine and blog until it closed. A charter member of C C Writers, she is contributing author to multiple anthology books and is writing her first book. She is Editor-in-Chief of this anthology.

RUTH ASHCRAFT MUNDAY has enjoyed conveying her thoughts via poetry and writing since childhood. After a fulfilling vocation as a registered nurse, Ruth felt the Lord calling her in a new direction. As only He can, the Lord blended her many life experiences as a nurse to prepare her for continued ministry in the community. With a special place in her heart for those struggling with grief, Ruth offers support and unique ideas for helping bereaved family members find positive ways to cope. Ever the aspiring author, Ruth has written and self-published three books.

DOYNE PHILLIPS is the Co-founder, Charter Member, and past Vice President of Collierville Christian Writers. He has contributed short stories to ten of C C Writers' eleven anthologies. He was also Co-founder and Managing Editor of *Southern Writers Magazine*, where he wrote numerous articles and over 230 blogs for their online site.

BARBARA RAGSDALE is an award-winning writer in short stories. She is published in *Forever Young*, three Chicken Soup for the Soul anthologies and multiple short-story collections published by CC Writers. Her story "A Walking Miracle" is published in Guideposts' *Miracles Do Happen*. Her poem "Final Moments" was published in *Can,Sir! Moments*. She was a columnist and staff writer for *Southern Writers Magazine*. When not writing, she is an exercise instructor with the Silver Sneakers program.

NANCY ROE has self-published eight books. *The Accident* won the Gold Quill Award, and *Butterfly Premonitions* won First Place for the first chapter. Nancy is a member of Sisters in Crime, The League of Utah Writers, and Newsletter Chair of the Newcomers Club of the Greater Park City Area.

DEBORAH SPRINKLE has written three romantic suspense novels that together make up the series Trouble in Pleasant Valley. She's won many awards, including one for a short story called *Progressive Dinner*, which is the inspiration for her new mystery series set in Washington, Missouri. Connect with Deborah at https://authordeborahsprinkle.com/.

ANNETTE G. TEEPE is a writer, scientist, educator, hiker, and life-long learner. Her passion is teaching others through her writing and speaking skills. She hopes to inspire future generations of scientists by publishing science topic books for elementary and middle school students. She is a member of the Bartlett Christian Writers group, the Collierville Christian Writers group, and the National Association for Science Writers.

JAN WERTZ is enjoying retirement life by turning her imagination loose as a writer, photographer, and traveler. One of her travel addictions is to sign on as a tourist with a storm chasing expert and his tour guides. A DAR, her writing frequently includes her family memoirs.

Also by C C WRITERS

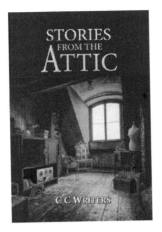